Car
The Wolv

Also by David Brian

The Strange Case at Misty Ridge

Dark Albion

Kaleen Rae and Other Weird Tales

The Cthulhu Child

The Damnation Game

The Boy on the Beach

Gloop!

Lonely is the Night

Carmilla: A Dark Fugue

Big Bad

Carmilla

The Wolves of Styria

Joseph Sheridan Le Fanu

And

David Brian

Night-Flyer

Carmilla: The Wolves of Styria

© 2011 David Brian

The right of David Brian to be identified as the Author of The Work has been asserted by him in accordance with the Copyright, Designs and Patents Act 1988.

All rights reserved. No part of this publication may be Reproduced, stored in or introduced to a retrieval system, or Transmitted, in any form, or by any means (electronic, mechanical, Photocopying, recording or otherwise) without the prior written permission of the copyright owner, except for brief quotation in reviews. Any person who does any unauthorized act in relation to this publication may be liable to criminal prosecution and civil claims for damages.

ISBN-13: 978-1481952217
ISBN-10: 1481952218

First published in 2011 by Night-Flyer Publishing

This book is dedicated to

Brian Frank Butlin.

Those who knew you described you as one of the best.

To me, you were always the best.

Sometimes, in order to clean up a mess, it is necessary to get your own hands dirty.
             General Spielsdorf.

Prologue

Upon a paper attached to the Narrative which follows, that most knowledgeable of Occult investigators, Doctor Martin Hesselius has written a rather elaborate note, which he accompanies with a reference to his Essay on the strange subject which the following collected papers serve to illuminate.

These most mysterious subjects, he treats in that Essay with his usual learning and acumen, and with remarkable directness and condensation. It shall, I am sure, form but one volume of the series of that extraordinary man's collected papers.

As I publish the case in this volume, simply to interest the "laity", I shall hold back nothing from the contributors who relate it, and after due consideration I have decided to abstain from presenting any summary of the learned Doctor's reasoning, or indeed to make any further comment on a subject which he describes as "involving, probably some of the profoundest arcane of our dual existence, and its intermediates."

I was anxious on discovering this paper, to reopen the correspondence commenced by Doctor Hesselius, so many years earlier, with one of the central protagonists in this happening, a young woman named Laura Bennett, who was as clever and truthful as any informant seems ever to have been. Much to my regret, however, I found that she had died in the interval. Doctor Hesselius himself wrote a separate note, expressing deep regret at the lady's untimely passing, and within just a few short weeks of their correspondence.

She probably could have added little to her part of the Narrative, which is communicated in the following pages with, so far as I can pronounce, such conscientious particularity. It is though, a content which serves to be only further enhanced by the writings of other contributors to this bizarre set of occurrences.

Chapter 1

Correspondence from Laura Bennett, addressed to Doctor Hesselius. *March 6th, 1871*

In Styria, we, although by no means magnificent people, inhabit a castle, or schloss. A small income in that part of the world goes a great way. Eight or nine hundred a year does wonders. Scantily enough ours would have answered among wealthy people at home. My father is English, and I am proud to bear an English name, although I had never seen England. But here, in this most lonely and primitive place, where everything is so marvellously cheap, I really don't see how ever so much more money would at all materially add to our comforts, or even luxuries.

My father was in the Austrian service, and retired upon a pension and his patrimony, purchasing this feudal residence and the small estate on which it stands, a bargain.

Nothing can be more picturesque, or indeed more solitary. It stands on a slight eminence in a forest. The road, very old and narrow, passes in front of its drawbridge, never raised in my time, and its moat, stocked with perch, and sailed over by many swans, and floating on its surface white fleets of water lilies.

Over all this the schloss shows its many-windowed front; its towers, and its Gothic chapel.

The forest opens in an irregular and very picturesque glade before its gate, and at the right a steep Gothic bridge carries the road over a stream that winds in deep shadow through the wood, passing the remains of an even more antiquated chapel, which sits amongst a sea of forsaken tombstones.

To the rear of our property, and not easily viewed from the occupied rooms within the schloss, there are two large areas of land, cleared some sixty years previous; one field is arable and used to grow maize, the other is kept for grazing beasts of burden.

I have said that this is a very lonely place. Judge whether I say truth. Looking from the hall door towards the road, the forest in which our castle stands extends fifteen miles to the right and twelve to the left. The nearest inhabited village is about seven English miles to the left. The nearest inhabited schloss of any historic associations is that of General Spielsdorf, nearly twenty miles away to the right.

I have said "the nearest *inhabited* village," because there is, only three miles westward, that is to say in the direction of General Spielsdorf's schloss, a ruined village, with its quaint little church, now roofless, in the aisle of which are the mouldering tombs of the proud family of Karnstein, now extinct, who once owned the equally desolate chateau which, in the thick of the forest, overlooks the silent ruins of the town.

Respecting the cause of the desertion of this striking and melancholy spot, there is a legend which I shall relate to you another time.

The smattering of modest dwellings that exist, in and around the forest, are mostly occupied by humble people who scrape a living from the land, though a few also house those who are employed in service in some capacity by my father Thomas Bennett.

I would tell now how very small the party who constitute the inhabitants of our castle is. I don't include servants, or those dependents who occupy rooms in the buildings attached to the schloss. Listen, and wonder! My father, who for sure is the kindest man on earth, but growing old, and I, whom at the time of which I write, numbered only nineteen years.

My father and I constitute the family at the schloss. My mother, a Styrian lady, died in my infancy, but I have been blessed with a good-natured governess who has been with me from, I might almost say, my infancy. I can not remember the time when her fat, benignant face was not a familiar picture in my memory.
This is Madame Perrodon, a native of Berne, whose care and good nature now in part compensated me the loss of my mother, whom I do not even remember it was so early I lost her. She makes up a third at our little dinner party. There is a fourth, Mademoiselle De Lafontaine, a lady such as you term, I believe, a "finishing governess." This is a position that the Mademoiselle De Lafontaine greatly prides herself on. Her dark hair is always

worn high in a tight bun, whilst equally tight corsets squeeze her trim waist, and at the same time serve to accentuate her ample bosom. She is always of stern countenance, which I find unfortunate, because with her high cheek bones and piercing blue eyes she could surely be a most handsome woman, if she would but allow herself the privilege of a smile. She speaks both French and German. Madame Perrodon, French and broken English, to which my father and I add English, which, partly to prevent its becoming a lost language among us, and partly from patriotic motives, we speak every day. The consequence can be a babble, at which strangers often choose to laugh, although for this I make no excuses. For as I have previously stated, both my father and I share a deep patriotism for the homeland. There are two or three young lady friends besides, pretty nearly of my own age, who are but occasional visitors, for longer or shorter terms; and these visits I, on occasion, return.

These are regular social resources; but mainly consisting of chance visits from "neighbours" of only five or six leagues distance. My life is, notwithstanding, a rather solitary one, I can assure you.

My gouvernantes have just so much control over me as you might conjecture such sage persons would have in the case of a rather spoiled girl, whose only parent allowed her pretty nearly her own way in everything.

The first occurrence in my existence which produced a terrible impression upon my mind, which, in fact, never has been effaced, was one of the very earliest incidents of my life which I can recollect. Some people will think it so trifling that it should not be recorded here, you will understand however, that the mere fact I can still recall it so clearly, even at this late stage, echoes just how deeply it has imbedded itself into my memory. And you will see, by-and-by, just why I mention it.

The nursery, as it was called, though I had it all to myself, was a large room in the upper story of the castle, with a steep oak roof. I could not have been more than six years old, when one night I awoke, and looking round the room from my bed, failed to see the nursery maid. Neither was there any sign of my nurse within the room; and I thought myself alone. I was not frightened, for I was one of those happy children who are studiously kept in ignorance of ghost stories, of fairy tales, and of all such lore as makes us cover up our heads when the door cracks suddenly, or the flicker of an expiring candle makes the shadow of a bedpost dance upon the wall, nearer to our faces. I was vexed and insulted at finding myself, as I conceived, neglected, and I began to whimper, preparatory to a hearty bout of roaring; when to my surprise I saw a solemn, but very pretty face looking at me from the side of the bed. It was that of a young lady who was kneeling, with her hands under the coverlet. I looked at her with a kind of pleased wonder, and ceased whimpering. She caressed me with her hands, and lay down beside me on the bed, drawing me towards her. Smiling, I felt immediately delightfully soothed, and fell asleep again. I was awakened by a sensation as if two needles ran into my breast very deep at the same moment, and I cried loudly. The lady started back, with her eyes fixed on me, and then slipped down upon the floor and, as I thought, hid herself under the bed.

I was now for the first time frightened, and I yelled with all my might and main. Nurse, nursery maid and housekeeper, all came running in, and upon hearing my story they made light of it, soothing me all they could. But child as I was, I could perceive that their faces were pale with an unwonted look of anxiety, and I saw them look under the bed and about the room, peep under tables and pluck open cupboards. The housekeeper whispered to the nurse: "Lay your hand along that hollow in the bed; for someone *did* lie there, as sure as you did not; the place is still warm."

I remember the nursery maid petting me, and all three examining my chest, where I told them I felt the puncture, and pronouncing that there was no sign visible that any such thing had happened to me.

The housekeeper and the two other servants who were in charge of the nursery, remained sitting up all night; and from that time a servant always sat up in the nursery, until I was about fourteen.

I was very nervous for a long time after this. A doctor was called in, he was pallid and elderly. How well I remember his long saturnine face, slightly pitted with smallpox, and his chestnut wig. For a good while, every second day he came and gave me medicine, which of course I hated.

The morning after I saw this apparition, I was in a state of terror, and could not bear to be left alone, daylight though it was, for a moment.

I remember my father coming up and standing at my bedside, talking cheerfully, asking the nurse a number of questions, and laughing very heartily at one of the answers. He patted me on the shoulder, kissed me, and told me not to be frightened, that it was nothing but a dream and could not hurt me.

However, I was not comforted, for I knew the visit of the strange woman was *not* a dream; and I was awfully frightened.

I was a little consoled by the nursery maid assuring me that it was she who had come and looked at me, and lain down beside me in the bed, and that I must have been half-dreaming not to have known her face. But this, though supported by the nurse, did not quite satisfy me.

I remembered, in the course of that day, a venerable old man in a black cassock, coming into the room with the nurse and housekeeper, talking a little to them, and very kindly to me. His face was very sweet and gentle, and he told me they were going to pray, and joined my hands together, and desired me to say, softly, while they were praying, "Lord hear all good prayers for us, and for Jesus' sake." I think these were the very words, for I often repeated them to myself, and my nurse used for years to make me say them in my prayers.

I remembered so well the thoughtful sweet face of that white-haired old man, in his black cassock, as he stood in that rude, lofty, brown room, with the clumsy furniture of a fashion three hundred years old about him, and the scanty light entering its shadowy atmosphere through the small lattice. He knelt, and the three women with him, and he prayed aloud with an earnest quavering voice for, what appeared to me, a long time. I forget all my life preceding that event, and for some time after it all is obscure too, but the scenes I have just described stand out vivid as the isolated pictures of the phantasmagoria surrounded by darkness. As to just why this should be, I did not know, but it is a memory that has pervaded my mind almost every day since its occurrence. Pray I had known then, of the portent of doom contained within my earlier visitation.

Chapter 2

Correspondence from Laura Bennett, addressed to Doctor Hesselius. *March 6th, 1871*

The day it started, I remember well. It was a Saturday, and the date was July 7th in the year of our Lord *1860*. It was a day which brought events of a most joyous nature to our home, although the good was first preceded by some very sad news indeed. Also, on this day, I witnessed an occurrence so strange that it will require faith in my veracity, in order for your good self, and indeed any other who may later read these words, to believe my story. It is not only true, nevertheless, but truth of which I have been an eyewitness.

The whole day had been exceptionally warm, and the passing of the hours had led to a sweet summer evening. My father had asked me, as he sometimes did, to take a little ramble with him along that beautiful forest vista, which I have mentioned before as lying in front of the schloss.

"General Spielsdorf cannot come to us as soon as I had hoped," said my father, as we pursued our walk.

He was to have paid us a visit of some weeks, and we had expected his arrival the next day. The General was to have brought with him a young lady, his betrothed; Mademoiselle Rheinfeldt, whom I had never seen, but whom I had heard described as a very charming woman, and in whose society I had promised myself many happy days. I was more disappointed than a young lady living in a town, or a bustling neighbourhood can possibly imagine. This visit, and the new acquaintance it promised, had furnished my daydreams for many weeks, for although the good General Spielsdorf was a man not far short of my fathers years, Mademoiselle Rheinfeldt was barely more than a girl herself, being some six months short of celebrating her twenty first birthday. Further still, the excitement of discussing with Bertha their upcoming nuptials, for she and the General had been planning a wedding in the fall, was, as I am sure you can imagine, something glorious for a girl of my age.

"And how soon does he come?" I had asked.

"Not till autumn. Not for two months or more, I dare say," he answered. "And I am very glad now, dear, that you never knew Mademoiselle Rheinfeldt."

"And why?" I asked, both mortified and curious.

"Because the poor young lady is dead!" he replied. "I am sorry I did not inform you of this most tragic event any sooner, but you were not in the room when I received the General's letter this evening."

I was very much shocked. General Spielsdorf had mentioned in his first letter, six or seven weeks before, that she was not so well as he would wish her, but there was nothing to suggest the remotest suspicion of danger.

"Here is the General's letter," Father said, handing it to me. "I am afraid he is in great affliction; the letter appears to me to have been written very nearly in distraction."

We sat down on a rude bench, under a group of magnificent lime trees. The sun was setting with its entire melancholy splendour behind the sylvan horizon, and the stream that flows beside our home, and passes under the steep old bridge I have mentioned, wound through many a group of noble trees, almost at our feet, reflecting in its current the fading crimson of the sky. General Spielsdorf's letter was so extraordinary, so vehement, and in some places so self-contradictory, that I read it twice over—the second time aloud to my father—and was still unable to account for it, except by supposing that grief had unsettled his mind.

It said, "I have lost my darling beloved and, as such, I am truly lost. It was doubtful that a military man such as I could ever, or indeed should ever, have expected to find true tenderness, for sure now I am empty inside, having felt such a love for her, only to have it cruelly ripped away. During the last days of dear Bertha's illness, I was not able to write to you. Before then I had no idea of her danger. I have lost her, and now learn *all*, too late. She died in the peace of freedom, having found someone prepared to love her for whom she was, and in the glorious hope of a blessed futurity.

"The fiend who betrayed our infatuated hospitality has done it all. I thought I was receiving into my house innocence, gaiety, a charming companion for my lost Bertha. Heavens! Such a fool I have been! I thank God my beloved died without a suspicion of the cause of her sufferings. She is gone without so much as conjecturing the nature of her illness and the accursed passion of the agent of all this misery.

"There are many wonders that exist within the boundaries of this world, upon which the laity might confer the title of 'monster'. I, too, was once as blind to the nature of reality as those who believe that there exists the Lord Almighty above, humankind below, and precious little in between. Thankfully, my beautiful Bertha was able to open the eyes of this old soldier, and show me the goodness that exists within this world. But there are monsters, and I devote my remaining days to tracking and extinguishing a true horror. I am told I may hope to accomplish my righteous and merciful purpose. At present there is scarcely a gleam of light to guide me. I curse my conceited incredulity, my despicable affectation of superiority, my blindness, my obstinacy—all—too late. I cannot write or talk collectedly now, I am distracted. As soon as I shall have a little recovered, I mean to devote myself for a time to enquiry. First, though, I must travel north. Bertha, all too often spoke of her kin, and I know she still has family there. A journey of some fifty leagues, I can but hope that these Rheinfeldt men greet me with accord, and that they will help me seek retribution for this crime. Some time in the autumn, two months hence, or maybe earlier if I live, I will see you—that is, if you permit me; I will then tell you all that I scarce dare put upon paper now. Farewell. Pray for me, dear friend."

In these terms ended this strange letter. Though I had never seen Bertha Rheinfeldt, my eyes filled with tears at the sudden intelligence; I was startled, as well as profoundly disappointed.

The sun had now set, and it was twilight by the time I returned the General's letter to my father.

It was a soft clear evening, and we loitered, speculating upon the possible meanings of the violent and incoherent sentences which I had just been reading. We had nearly a mile to walk before reaching the road that passes the schloss in front, and by this time the moon was shining brilliantly. At the drawbridge we met Madame Perrodon and Mademoiselle De Lafontaine, who had come out, without their bonnets, to enjoy the exquisite moonlight.

We heard their voices gabbling in animated dialogue as we approached. We joined them at the drawbridge and turned about to admire with them the beautiful scene.

The glade through which we had just walked lay before us. At our left the narrow road wound away under clumps of lordly trees and was lost to sight amid the thickening forest. At the right the same road crosses the steep and picturesque bridge, near which stands a ruined tower which once guarded that pass; and beyond the bridge an abrupt eminence rises, covered with trees, and showing in the shadows some grey ivy-clustered rocks.

Over the sward and low grounds a thin film of mist was stealing like smoke, marking the distances with a transparent veil; and here and there we could see the river faintly flashing in the moonlight.

No softer, sweeter scene could be imagined. The news I had just heard made it melancholy; but nothing could disturb its character of profound serenity and the enchanted glory and vagueness of the prospect.

My father, who enjoyed the picturesque, and I, stood looking in silence over the expanse beneath us. The two good governesses, standing a little way behind us, discoursed upon the scene, and were eloquent upon the moon.

Madame Perrodon was fat, middle-aged, and romantic, and talked and sighed poetically. Mademoiselle De Lafontaine—in right of her father who was a German, assumed to be psychological, metaphysical, and something of a mystic—now declared that when the moon shone with a light so intense, it was well known that it indicated a special spiritual activity. The effect of the full moon in such a state of brilliancy was manifold.

It acted on dreams, it acted on lunacy, it acted on nervous people, and it had marvellous physical influences connected with life. Mademoiselle related, in her normal aloof manner, that her cousin, who was mate of a merchant ship, having taken a nap on deck on such a night, lying on his back, with his face full in the light of the moon, had awakened from a dream of an old woman clawing him by the cheek, with his features horribly drawn to one side, and his countenance had never quite recovered its equilibrium.

"The moon, this night," she said, "is full of idyllic and magnetic influence—and see, when you look behind you at the front of the schloss how all its windows flash and twinkle with that silvery splendour, as if unseen hands had lighted up the rooms to receive fairy guests," she lectured, in such a way as though her every spoken word was fact.

There are indolent styles of the spirits in which, indisposed to talk ourselves, the talk of others is pleasant to our listless ears; and I gazed on, pleased with the tinkle of the ladies' conversation.

"I have gotten into one of my moping moods tonight," said my father, after a silence, and quoting Shakespeare, whom, by way of keeping up our English, he used to read aloud, he said:

"*In truth I know not why I am so sad. It wearies me: you say it wearies you; but how I got it—came by it.*' "I forget the rest. But I feel as if some great misfortune is hanging over us. I suppose the poor General's afflicted letter has something to do with it."

At this moment, the unwonted sound of carriage wheels and many hoofs upon the road arrested our attention.

They seemed to be approaching from the high ground overlooking the bridge, and very soon the equipage emerged from that point. Two horsemen first crossed the bridge, and then came a carriage drawn by four horses, and two men rode behind.

It seemed to be the travelling carriage of a person of rank; and we were all immediately absorbed in watching this very unusual spectacle. It became, in a few moments, greatly more interesting, for just as the carriage had passed the summit of the steep bridge, one of the leaders, taking fright, communicated his panic to the rest, and after a plunge or two, the whole team broke into a wild gallop together, and dashing between the horsemen who rode in front, came thundering along the road towards us with the speed of a hurricane.

The excitement of the scene was made more painful by the clear, long-drawn screams of a female voice from the carriage window.

We all advanced in curiosity and horror; me rather in silence, the rest with various ejaculations of terror.

Our suspense did not last long. Just before you reach the castle drawbridge, on the route they were coming, there stands by the roadside a magnificent lime tree. On the other stands an ancient stone cross, at sight of which the horses, now going at a pace that was perfectly frightful, swerved so as to bring the wheel over the projecting roots of the tree.

I knew what was coming. I covered my eyes, unable to see it out, and turned my head away; at the same moment I heard a cry from my lady friends, who had gone on a little.

Curiosity opened my eyes, and I saw a scene of utter confusion. Two of the horses were on the ground, the carriage lay upon its side with two wheels in the air; the men were busy removing the traces, and a lady, with a commanding air and figure, had got out, and stood with clasped hands, raising the handkerchief that was in them every now and then to her eyes. Through the carriage door was a young lady who appeared to be lifeless. My dear old father was already beside the elder lady, with his hat in his hand, evidently tendering his aid and the resources of his schloss. The lady did not appear to hear him, or to have eyes for anything but the slender girl who was being placed against the slope of the bank.

I approached; the young lady was apparently stunned, but she was certainly not dead. My father, who piqued himself on being something of a physician, had just had his fingers on her wrist and assured the lady, who declared herself her mother, that her pulse, though faint and irregular, was undoubtedly still distinguishable. The lady clasped her hands and looked upward, as if in a momentary transport of gratitude, but immediately she broke out again in that theatrical way which is I believe, natural to some people.

She was what is called a fine looking woman for her time of life, and must have been handsome; she was tall, but not thin, and dressed in black velvet, and looked rather pale, but with a proud and commanding countenance, though now agitated strangely.

"Who has ever been so born to calamity?" I heard her say, with clasped hands, as I came up. "Here am I, on a journey of life and death, in prosecuting which to lose an hour is possibly to lose all. My child will not have recovered sufficiently to resume her route for who can say how long. I must leave her; I cannot, nor dare not, delay. How far on, sir, can you tell me, is the nearest village? I must leave her there; and shall not see my darling, or even hear of her till my return, three months hence."

I plucked my father by the coat, and whispered earnestly in his ear:

"Oh! Papa, pray ask her to stay with us—it would be so delightful. Do, pray."

"If Madame will entrust her child to the care of my daughter, and of her good gouvernante, Madame Perrodon, and permit her to remain as our guest, under my charge, until her return, it will confer a distinction and an obligation upon us, and we shall treat her with all the care and devotion which so sacred a trust deserves."

"I cannot do that, sir; it would be to task your kindness and chivalry too cruelly," said the lady, distractedly.

"It would, on the contrary, be to confer on us a very great kindness at the moment when we most need it. My daughter has just been disappointed by a cruel misfortune, in a visit from which she had long anticipated a great deal of happiness. If you confide this young lady to our care it will be her best consolation. The nearest village on your route is distant and affords no such inn as you could think of placing your daughter at; you cannot allow her to continue her journey for any considerable distance without danger. If, as you say, you cannot suspend your journey, you must part with her tonight, and nowhere could you do so with more honest assurances of care and tenderness than here."

There was something in this lady's air and appearance, so distinguished and even imposing, and in her manner so engaging, as to impress one, quite apart from the dignity of her equipage, with a conviction that she was a person of consequence.

By this time the carriage was replaced in its upright position, and the horses, quite tractable, in the traces again.

The lady threw on her daughter a glance, which I fancied was not quite as affectionate as one might have anticipated from the beginning of the scene. Then she beckoned slightly to my father, withdrew two or three steps with him out of hearing, and talked to him with a fixed and stern countenance, not at all like that with which she had hitherto spoken.

I was filled with wonder that my father did not seem to perceive the change, and also unspeakably curious to learn what it could be that she was speaking, almost in his ear, with so much earnestness and rapidity.

Two or three minutes at most I think she remained thus employed, then she turned, and a few steps brought her to where her daughter lay, supported by Madame Perrodon. She knelt beside the girl for a moment and whispered, as Madame supposed, a little benediction in her ear, and then did the most strange of things. Withdrawing a small glass vial, containing a liquid which appeared to be perfume, from within her velvet lined pocket, she uncorked the bottle before proceeding to shower the stricken girl with the fluid, covering her person from head to toe. Once she had finished bestowing her strange gift upon the girl she hastily kissed her face, before turning away and stepping back into her carriage. The door was closed, and the footmen in stately liveries jumped up behind. The outriders spurred on, the postilions cracked their whips, and the horses plunged and broke suddenly into a furious canter that threatened soon again to become a gallop, and the carriage whirled away, followed at the same rapid pace by the two horsemen in the rear.

Chapter 3

Correspondence from Laura Bennett, addressed to Doctor Hesselius. *March 6th, 1871*

We followed the cortège with our eyes, until it was swiftly lost to sight in the misty wood; and the very sound of the hoofs and the wheels died away in the silent night air.

Nothing at that point remained to assure us that the adventure had not been an illusion, but for the young lady, who just at that moment opened her eyes. I could not see, for her face was turned from me, but she raised her head, evidently looking about her, and I heard a very sweet voice ask complainingly, "Where is Mamma?"

Our good Madame Perrodon answered tenderly, and added some comfortable assurances.

I then heard her ask: "Where am I? What is this place?" and after that she said, "I don't see the carriage; and Matska, where is she?"

Madame answered all her questions in so far as she understood them, and gradually the young lady remembered how the misadventure came about, and was glad to hear that no one in, or in attendance on the carriage was hurt; and on learning that her mamma had left her here, till her return in about three months, she wept.

I was going to add my consolations to those of Madame Perrodon when Mademoiselle De Lafontaine placed her hand upon my arm, saying:

"Don't approach, one at a time is as much as she can at present converse with; a very little excitement would possibly overpower her now."

As soon as she is comfortably in bed, I thought, I will run up to her room and see her.

My father in the meantime had instructed that a servant on horseback be sent for the physician, who lived about two leagues away; and also that a bedroom be prepared for the young lady's reception.

The stranger now rose, and leaning on Madame's arm, walked slowly towards the drawbridge that led into the castle gate, our small group forming a cortege behind them.

It was at this point, that for sure the evening's strangest of happenings occurred. We were barely a stone's throw from the drawbridge, when a sound, much like the distant rolling of thunder, signalled that once again something was approaching from the high ground. In unison, we turned, only to behold a sight the like of which I will never forget.

Down from the hills, and running out onto the bridge, there appeared a wolf. Now I make no claim to having been an expert on such animals, indeed my previous experience consisted of only ever before having seen two of these most beguiling of creatures. They are rare in these parts now, and on both previous occasions it had been but the briefest of glimpses, viewed from some considerable distance. However, even allowing for my lack of knowledge of such beasts, I recognised the fact that this animal was huge, being easily big enough to have taken down a stallion, without assistance from other members of its pack.

I opened my mouth to speak; I was both excited and alarmed at being in such close proximity to this fascinating and equally frightening creature. However, my silence was sustained by Mademoiselle De Lafontaine's grip upon my forearm. A grip which grew suddenly tighter, as with her other hand she pointed back towards the hills. Our little group fell as silent as it had become still, not a one of us daring to move. We watched in awe, and I dare say no small amount of fear, as running down from the hilltops, under the light of a silver moon, there appeared six more wolves. They raced out onto the road, and then across the bridge, and although slightly smaller in stature than the first black beast, every one and all looked a most formidable creature.

Within an instant they had passed, trailing off in the same direction the carriage cortège had previously taken. It took us some moments before any of us actually found our voices, and then we broke into an excitable babble, each one of us seeking to offer our own explanation as to what could have possibly brought these animals this close to our home.

Various hypotheses were offered up to account for the appearance of the wolves, and it was an event we would further discuss many times over the coming days. Yet thinking back to these events now, although it was not noticed by me at the time, I am sure that our young visitor did not partake of discussion about the beasts, at least not on that first night of her arrival at our schloss.

Chapter 4

Correspondence from Laura Bennett, addressed to Doctor Hesselius. *March 6th, 1871*

After the passing of the wolves, we returned with our guest to the comfort of our schloss. In the hall, servants waited to receive her, and she was conducted forthwith to her room.

The room we usually sat in as our drawing room is long, having four windows which looked out over the moat and drawbridge, upon the forest scene which I have previously described.

It is furnished in old carved oak with large carved cabinets, and the chairs are cushioned with crimson Utrecht velvet. The walls are covered with tapestry, and surrounded with great gold frames, the figures being as large as life, in ancient and very curious costume, and the subjects represented are hunting, hawking, and generally festive. It is not too stately to be extremely comfortable; and here we had our tea, for with his usual patriotic leanings, my father insisted that the national beverage should make its appearance regularly with our coffee and chocolate.

We sat here this night, and with candles lighted, were talking over the adventure of the evening.

Madame Perrodon and Mademoiselle De Lafontaine were both of our party. The young stranger had hardly lain down in her bed when she sank into a deep sleep; and those ladies had left her in the care of a servant.

After more conjecture about the passing of the wolves, and in such a close proximity to our home, our thoughts turned once again to our visitor.

"How do you like our guest?" I asked Madame. "Tell me all about her?"

"I like her extremely," answered Madame, "she is, I almost think, the prettiest creature I ever saw; about your age, and so gentle and nice."

"She is absolutely beautiful," threw in Mademoiselle, who had peeped for a moment into the stranger's room.

"And such a sweet voice!" added Madame Perrodon.

"Did you remark a woman in the carriage, after it was set up again, who did not get out," inquired Mademoiselle, "but only looked from the window?"

"No, we had not seen her," I replied, as Madame shook her head in agreement.

Then, Mademoiselle described a hideous black woman, with a sort of coloured turban on her head, who was gazing all the time from the carriage window; nodding and grinning derisively towards the ladies, with gleaming eyes and large white eyeballs, and her teeth set as if in fury.

"Did you remark what an ill-looking pack of men the servants were?" asked Madame.

"Yes," said my father, who had just come in, "ugly, and hang-dog looking fellows as ever I beheld in my life. I hope they mayn't rob the poor lady in the forest. They are clever rogues, however; they got everything to rights in a minute."

"I dare say they are worn out with too long travelling," said Madame. "Besides looking wicked, their faces were so strangely lean, dark, and sullen. I am very curious, but I dare say the young lady will tell you all about it tomorrow, if she is sufficiently recovered."

"I don't think she will," said my father, with a mysterious smile, and a little nod of his head, as if he knew more about it than he cared to tell us.

This made us all the more inquisitive as to what had passed between him and the lady in the black velvet, in the brief but earnest interview that had immediately preceded her departure.

We were scarcely alone, when I entreated him to tell me. He did not need much pressing.

"There is no particular reason why I should not tell you. She expressed a reluctance to trouble us with the care of her daughter, saying she was in delicate health, and nervous, but not subject to any kind of seizure—she volunteered that—nor to any illusion; being in fact perfectly sane."

"How very odd it is that she should have said all that!" I interpolated. "It was so unnecessary."

"At all events it *was* said," he laughed, "and as you wish to know all that passed, which was indeed very little, I tell you. She then said, 'I am making a long journey of *vital* importance—she emphasized the word—rapid and secret; I shall return for my child in three months; in the meantime, she will be silent as to who we are, whence we come, and whither we are travelling.' That is all she said. She spoke very pure French. When she said the word 'secret,' she paused for a few seconds, looking sternly, her eyes fixed on mine. I fancy she makes a great point of that. You saw how quickly she was gone. I hope I have not done a very foolish thing, in taking charge of the young lady."

For my part I was delighted. I was longing to see and talk to her; and only waiting till Doctor Spielberg, who had been called to examine our guest, should give me his leave. You, who live in towns, can have no idea how great an event the introduction of a new friend is, in such solitude as surrounded us.

The doctor did not arrive till nearly one o'clock; but I could no more have gone to my bed and slept, than I could have overtaken, on foot the carriage in which the princess in black velvet had driven away.

When the physician came down to the drawing room, it was to report very favourably upon his patient. She was now sitting up, her pulse quite regular, apparently perfectly well. She had sustained no injury, and the little shock to her nerves, brought on by her mother's exodus, and the incident with the wolves, had passed away quite harmlessly. There could be no harm certainly in my seeing her, if we both wished it; and, with this permission I sent forthwith, to know whether she would allow me to visit her for a few minutes in her room.

The servant returned immediately to say that she desired nothing more.

You may be sure I was not long in availing myself of this permission.

Our visitor lay in one of the handsomest rooms in the schloss. It was perhaps a little stately. There was a sombre piece of tapestry opposite the foot of the bed, representing Cleopatra with the asps to her bosom; and other solemn classic scenes were displayed, a little faded, upon the other walls. But there was gold carving, and rich and varied colour enough in the other decorations of the room to more than redeem the gloom of the old tapestry.

There were candles at the bedside. She was sitting up; her slender pretty figure enveloped in the soft silk dressing gown, embroidered with flowers, and lined with thick quilted silk, which her mother had thrown over her feet as she lay upon the ground.

What was it that, as I reached the bedside and had just begun my little greeting, struck me dumb in a moment, and made me recoil a step or two from before her? I will tell you.

I saw the very face which had visited me in my childhood at night, which remained so fixed in my memory, and on which I had for so many years so often ruminated with horror, when no one suspected of what I was thinking.

It was pretty, even beautiful; and when I first beheld it, wore the same melancholy expression.

But this almost instantly lighted into a strange fixed smile of recognition.

There was a silence of fully a minute, and then at length she spoke; I could not.

"How wonderful!" she exclaimed. "Twelve years ago, I saw your face in a dream, and it has haunted me ever since."

"Yes, wonderful indeed!" I repeated, overcoming with an effort the horror that had for a time suspended my utterances. "Twelve years ago, in vision or reality, I certainly saw you. I could not forget your face. It has remained before my eyes ever since."

Her smile had softened. Whatever I had fancied strange in it, was gone, and it and her dimpling cheeks were now delightfully pretty and intelligent.

I felt reassured, and continued more in the vein which hospitality indicated, to bid her welcome and to tell her how much pleasure her accidental arrival had given us all, and especially what a happiness it was to me.

I took her hand as I spoke. I was a little shy, as lonely people are, but the situation made me eloquent, and even bold. She pressed my hand, laid hers upon it, and her eyes glowed, as looking hastily into mine, she smiled again, and blushed.

She answered my welcome very prettily. I sat down beside her, still wondering, and she said:

"I must tell you my vision about you; it is so very strange that you and I should have had, each of the other so vivid a dream, that each should have seen, I you and you me, looking as we do now when of course we both were mere children. I was a child, about six years old, and I awoke from a confused and troubled dream, and found myself in a room, unlike my nursery; wainscoted clumsily in some dark wood, with cupboards and bedsteads, chairs and benches placed about it. The beds were, I thought, all empty, and the room itself without anyone but myself in it; and I, after looking about me for some time, and admiring especially an iron candlestick with two branches, which I should certainly know again, crept under one of the beds to reach the window: As I got from under the bed, I heard someone crying; and looking up, while I was still upon my knees, I saw you—most assuredly you—as I see you now. A beautiful young lady, with golden hair and large blue eyes, and lips—your lips—you, as you are here. Your looks won me; I climbed on the bed and put my arms about you, and I think we both fell asleep. I was aroused by a scream; you were sitting up screaming. I was frightened and slipped down upon the ground, and, it seemed to me, lost consciousness for a moment; and when I came to myself, I was again in my nursery at home. Your face I have never forgotten since. I could not be misled by mere resemblance. *You are* the lady whom I saw then."

It was now my turn to relate my corresponding vision, which I did to the undisguised wonder of my new acquaintance.

"I don't know which should be most afraid of the other," she said, again smiling. "If you were less pretty I think I should be very much afraid of you, but being as you are, and you and I both so young, I feel only that I have made your acquaintance twelve years ago and have already a right to your intimacy; at all events it does seem as if we were destined, from our earliest childhood, to be friends. I wonder whether you feel as strangely drawn towards me as I do to you; I have never had a friend—shall I find one now?" She sighed, and her fine dark eyes gazed passionately on me.

Now the truth is, I felt rather unaccountably towards the beautiful stranger. I did feel as she said, "drawn towards her," indeed, even looking upon her smiling face made my cheeks flush crimson, a feeling of shy reserve tugged inexplicably at my very being with every word she spoke to me. But there was also something of repulsion. In this ambiguous feeling however, the sense of attraction immensely prevailed. She interested and won me; she was so beautiful and so indescribably engaging.

I perceived now something of languor and exhaustion stealing over her, and hastened to bid her good night.

"The doctor thinks," I added, "that you ought to have a maid to sit up with you tonight; one of ours is waiting, and you will find her a very useful and quiet creature."

"How kind of you, but I could not sleep, I never could with an attendant in the room. I shan't require any assistance—and shall I confess my weakness, I am haunted with a terror of robbers. Our house was robbed once, and two servants murdered, so I always lock my door. It has become a habit—and you look so kind I know you will forgive me. I see there is a key in the lock."

She held me close in her pretty arms for a moment and whispered in my ear, "Good night, darling, it is very hard to part with you, but good night; tomorrow, but not early, I shall see you again."

She sank back on the pillow with a sigh, and her fine eyes followed me with a fond and melancholy gaze, and she murmured again, "Good night, dear friend."

Young people like, and even love, on impulse. I was flattered by the evident, though as yet undeserved, fondness she showed me. I liked the confidence with which she at once received me. She was determined that we should be very near friends, and this brought a smile of satisfaction to my face.

Next day came and we met again. I was delighted with my companion; that is to say, in many respects.

Her looks lost nothing in daylight—she was certainly the most beautiful creature I had ever seen, and the unpleasant remembrance of the face presented in my early dream, had lost the effect of the first unexpected recognition.

She confessed that she had experienced a similar shock on seeing me, and precisely the same faint antipathy that had mingled with my admiration of her. We now laughed together over our momentary horrors.

Chapter 5

A letter written by Doctor Alvinci, addressed to Baron Vordenburg. Dated *August 10th, 1860*

Dear Baron Vordenburg,

I write in the hope that you will remember meeting my good self; we were introduced at a garden party at the home of the Baroness von Waxensteini, almost three years ago.

It may help your memory of me if I tell you that I am a rather tall individual, standing several inches higher than the average Austrian male, a fact which you yourself commented on. The two of us spent some hours in conversation, in part because it became apparent we shared a number of similar interests, particularly in all subjects esoteric. Things, that if I might say, you are substantially more adept at than myself. Although I should also mention that since last we spoke I have had experience of what I believe to have been a revenant, and unfortunately that incident did not end at all well for the young lady involved. I can assure you that the situation, with which I am now confronted, far outweighs that which has gone before. It is for this very reason I write to you now, as I feel sure your expertise is needed in order to cleanse this district of a most despicable evil.

I am myself new to this area, having arrived a fortnight earlier, and only then at the behest of my good friend and colleague Doctor Spielberg. He knew of my interest in the arcane and he hoped, vainly as it transpired, that I may have been able to resolve the growing unpleasantness which surrounds us.

I will tell you now some of the strange and repugnant happenings which have been afflicting these lands, in the hope you may be able to offer some guidance as to how these matters should be proceeded with.

For several weeks now this district has been subjected to a most mysterious malady, one that for the most part, but not always, afflicts females, and usually then being girls within a certain range of ages. I myself had only been here for a number of days, when Doctor Spielberg suggested I accompany him on his rounds, as he was due that morning to visit Analiese Dorner, she being the young wife of a local swineherd, Bruno.

Analiese had, some days earlier, claimed to have woken from her sleep to find something heavy attached to her throat. She fought desperately to free herself, as she felt, in her words, "that the very life was being throttled out of her." Then, without any obvious reason, the fiend released her. Sitting upright, she saw a darkly dressed figure on the far side of the room, near the door. For one brief moment she thought that she saw a female face staring back at her from under the cowl, and just as quickly the apparition was gone. Analiese spent some minutes trying to wake her husband, a light sleeper, from his position on the bed beside her, but was unable to rouse him. And within just a short time, she felt a strange melancholy sweeping through her body, debilitating her strength, and she quickly lapsed into a deep, but fitful sleep.

Doctor Spielberg and I arrived at the Dorner's modest dwelling at just past midday; a worried looking Bruno greeted us upon our arrival. After a brief conversation, in which he largely despaired at his wife's continuing decline, we followed him inside to where his bedridden wife lay.

I must confess to having been shocked. Analiese, although bereft of any powders as would be expected for a woman of her standing, was a creature of beauty, or at least it was plain to see she once had been. A thick mop of brown hair, streaked with layers of blonde, adorned her crown and hung down over her shoulders. Her skin, though, had a pallid complexion, and though she smiled to acknowledge our arrival, her eyes remained dull and lifeless. I took hold of her wrist, to check her pulse, and found the touch clammy beyond reason. Analiese's heart beat steadily, although her breathing remained shallow. She had no fever. Neither did she suffer from any pockmarks, or other rashes elsewhere on her body. The only mark we did find was the tiniest blue bruise on her neck, at precisely the point where she described the strangulation as having commenced.

We questioned the woman at length, whereupon Analiese described in detail how since that first night, she had continued to suffer bouts of extremely fitful sleep, which usually involved dreams of a disturbing nature. She seemed highly reluctant to elaborate on the qualities of these dreams, although I sensed a degree of embarrassment in her coyness, rather than the fear of being forced to relive her nightmares. At my behest, my colleague took notes while I interviewed the woman, as he later did when we visited others in the area who had been similarly afflicted.

In total we attended the care of four patients, thus infected, in my first week here. I have to say there was a marked degree of similarity in each case. Each of those questioned exhibiting the same lack of vigour, and pallid complexion. They are also, as one, reluctant to elaborate on the nature of the dreams which accompany this illness.

Earlier this week, on the morning that Analiese, dressed in a pale blue dress with yellow stitching bordering the hems, was laid to rest, we attended the bedside of a young peasant girl named Katharina Bohm. A very sad case indeed given that the child was aged just sixteen years, even more so insofar as her father had raised her alone, the child's mother dying of fever some twelve years earlier.

Her papa, although reluctant to leave his sick child, had gained some work within the forest, and so had not returned home until after dark the previous night. Upon approaching their dwelling, the father heard his daughter moaning and calling out. Believing her to be in pain he strode out to their cottage, only to find upon entering a most despicable sight. Something dark was astride the girl, its head buried into her chest. According to the peasant, his daughter was indeed crying out, though not as he had first thought in pain, but rather in a way more akin to a couple alone.

Upon his entrance the beast withdrew from the girl, snarling and spitting as it did so. It became apparent that the fiend was a woman, at least of sorts. The black cloak that covered it fell open, revealing a naked female body, although the thing's face was twisted into a visage more suited to a demon escaped from Hell. The riding-hood seemed to move as though possessed of a life its own, shimmering and distorting as the she-fiend leapt from the bed. The peasant thought his life was done, but instead the creature, now on all fours, bounded past him, moving, he thought with an element of gracefulness, like some gigantic cat. Turning back to his daughter, he was distraught to find her nightgown hoisted high around her waist, and the upper fastenings loosed and pulled down, exposing her naked breasts. He covered the girl, and then attempted to wake her, but she never once again opened her eyes. Katharina died in the early hours of yesterday morning.

In this correspondence to you, I shall include copies of all notes taken, and also medical assessments carried out by my colleague and I, in the hope that these things may help illuminate an answer to this most grave matter. I have only ever read accounts of creatures such as the oupire, and succubus, hence I have no way of truly knowing if such demons can walk among us, although as you will have reasoned from my contacting you, I do consider this to be a likely explanation. Time is most certainly pressed in dealing with this situation, and I fear that without your expert guidance we may truly be lost. Therefore, I would beseech you to advise me forthwith as to how we may best proceed, in order that we are swiftly able to vanquish this onset of evil.

Sincerely yours,

Doctor Sebastian Alvinci

Chapter 6

Correspondence from Laura Bennett, addressed to Doctor Hesselius. *March 14th, 1871*

I told you that I was charmed with my new friend in most particulars.

There were some that did not please me so well, more so, if I am honest, during our early weeks together.

I shall begin by describing her. She was above the middle height of women. She was slender, finely proportioned and wonderfully graceful. Except that her movements were languid—very languid—indeed, there was nothing in her appearance to indicate an invalid. Her complexion was rich and brilliant; her features small and beautifully formed; her eyes large, dark, and lustrous; her hair was quite wonderful, I never saw hair so magnificently thick and long when it was down about her shoulders; I have often placed my hands under it and laughed with wonder at its weight. It was exquisitely fine and soft and in colour a rich very dark brown, with something of gold. I loved to let it down, tumbling with its own weight, as in her room, she lay back in her chair talking in her sweet low voice, I used to fold and braid it, and spread it out and play with it. Heavens! If I had but known all!

I said there were particulars which did not please me. I have told you that her confidence won me the first night I saw her, but I found that she exercised with respect to herself, her mother and her history, everything in fact connected with her life, plans and people, an ever wakeful reserve. I dare say I was unreasonable, perhaps I was wrong; I dare say I ought to have respected the solemn injunction laid upon my father by the stately lady in black velvet. But curiosity is a restless and unscrupulous passion, and no one girl can endure with patience, that hers should be baffled by another. What harm could it do anyone to tell me what I so ardently desired to know? Had she no trust in my good sense or honour? Why would she not believe me when I assured her, so solemnly, that I would not divulge one syllable of what she told me to any mortal breathing? There was coldness; it seemed to me, beyond her years, in her smiling melancholy persistent refusal to afford me the least ray of light.

I cannot say we quarrelled upon this point, for she would not quarrel upon any. It was of course, very unfair of me to press her, very ill-bred, but I really could not help it; and I might just as well have let it alone.

What she did tell me amounted, in my unconscionable estimation—to nothing.

It was all summed up in three very vague disclosures:

First—her name was Carmilla.

Second—her family was very ancient and noble.

Third—her home lay in the direction of the west.

She would not tell me the name of her family, nor their armorial bearings, or the name of their estate, nor even that of the country they lived in.

You are not to suppose that I worried her incessantly on these subjects. I watched opportunity and rather insinuated than urged my inquiries. Once or twice, indeed I did attack her more directly, but no matter what my tactics; utter failure was invariably the result. Reproaches and caresses were all lost upon her. But I must add this, that her evasion was conducted with so pretty a melancholy and deprecation, with so many and even passionate declarations of her liking for me, and trust in my honour, and with so many promises that I should at last know all, that I could not find it in my heart long to be offended with her.

She used to place her pretty arms about my neck, draw me to her, and laying her cheek to mine, murmur with her lips near my ear, "Dearest, your little heart is wounded; think me not cruel because I obey the irresistible law of my strength and weakness; if your dear heart is wounded, my wild heart bleeds with yours. In the rapture of my enormous humiliation I live in your warm life, and you shall die—die, sweetly die—into mine. I cannot help it; as I draw near to you, you, in your turn, will draw near to others, and learn the rapture of that cruelty, which yet is love; so, for a while, seek to know no more of me and mine, but trust me with all your loving spirit."

And when she had spoken such a rhapsody, she would press me more closely in her trembling embrace, and her lips in soft kisses gently glow upon my cheek.

Her agitations and her language were unintelligible to me.

From these foolish embraces, which were not a very frequent occurrence, I must allow that I, at first, used to wish to extricate myself, but my energies seemed to fail me. Her murmured words sounded like a lullaby in my ear and soothed my resistance into a trance, from which I only seemed to recover myself when she withdrew her arms.

In these mysterious moods I did not like her. I experienced a strange tumultuous yearning excitement that was pleasurable, ever more so, and yet mingled with a vague sense of fear and disgust. I had no distinct thoughts about her while such scenes lasted, but I was conscious of a love growing into adoration, and also of abhorrence. This I know is paradox, but I can make no other attempt to explain the feeling.

I now write, after an interval of more than ten years, with a trembling hand, with a confused and horrible recollection of certain occurrences and situations, in the ordeal through which I was unconsciously passing, though with a vivid and very sharp remembrance of the main current of my story. But, I suspect in all lives there are certain emotional scenes, those in which our passions have been most wildly and terribly roused, that are of all others the most vaguely and dimly remembered.

Sometimes, after an hour of apathy, my strange and beautiful companion would take my hand and hold it with a fond pressure, renewed again and again; blushing softly, gazing in my face with languid and burning eyes, and breathing so fast that her dress rose and fell with the tumultuous respiration. It was like the ardour of a lover; it embarrassed me, and equally it excited me; it was hateful and yet over-powering; and with gloating eyes she drew me to her, and her hot lips travelled along my cheek in kisses; she would whisper, almost in sobs, "You are mine, you *shall* be mine, you and I are one forever."

Then she had thrown herself back in her chair, with her small hands over her eyes, leaving me trembling.

"Are we related," I used to ask. "What can you mean by all this? I remind you perhaps of someone whom you love; but you must not, I hate it; I don't know you—I don't know myself when you look so and talk so."

She used to sigh at my vehemence, then turn away and drop my hand.

Respecting these very extraordinary manifestations, I strove in vain to form any satisfactory theory—I could not refer them to affection or trick. It was unmistakably the momentary breaking out of suppressed instinct and emotion. Was she, notwithstanding her mother's volunteered denial, subject to brief visitations of insanity, or were there here a disguise and a romance? I had read in old storybooks of such things. What if a boyish lover had found his way into the house, and sought to prosecute his suit in masquerade with the assistance of a clever old adventuress.

But there were many things against this hypothesis, highly interesting as it was to my vanity.

I could boast of no little attentions such as masculine gallantry delights to offer. Between these passionate moments there were long intervals of commonplace, of gaiety, of brooding reflection, during which I detected her eyes so full of melancholy fire, following me; at times I might have been as nothing to her. Except in these brief periods of mysterious excitement her ways were girlish; and there was always a languor about her, quite incompatible with a masculine system in a state of health.

In some respects her habits were odd. Perhaps not so singular in the opinion of a town dweller like you, as they appeared to us rustic people. She used to come down very late, generally not till one o'clock, she would then take a cup of chocolate, but eat nothing; we then went out for a walk, which was a mere saunter. She seemed almost immediately exhausted, and either returned to the schloss or sat on one of the benches that were placed here and there among the trees. This was a bodily languor in which her mind did not sympathize. She was always an animated talker, and very intelligent.

She sometimes alluded for a moment to her own home, or mentioned an adventure or situation, or an early recollection; which indicated a people of strange manners, and described customs of which we knew nothing. I gathered from these chance hints that her native country was much more remote than I had at first fancied.

As we sat thus one afternoon under the trees, a funeral passed us by. It was that of a pretty young girl, whom I had often seen, the daughter of one of the rangers of the forest. The poor man was walking behind the coffin of his darling; she was his only child, and he looked quite heartbroken. Peasants walking two-and-two came behind, they were singing a funeral hymn.

I rose to mark my respect as they passed, and joined in the hymn they were very sweetly singing.

My companion shook me a little roughly and I turned surprised.

She said brusquely, "Don't you perceive how discordant that is?"

"I think it very sweet, on the contrary," I answered, vexed at the interruption, and very uncomfortable, lest the people who composed the little procession should observe and resent what was passing.

I resumed, therefore, instantly, and was again interrupted.

"You pierce my ears," said Carmilla, almost angrily, and stopping her ears with her tiny fingers. "Besides, how can you tell that your religion and mine are the same; your forms wound me, and I hate funerals. What a fuss! Why you must die—*everyone* must die; and all are happier when they do. Come home."

"My father has gone on with the clergyman to the churchyard. I thought you knew she was to be buried today."

"She? I don't trouble my head about peasants. I don't know who *she* is!" answered Carmilla, with a flash from her fine eyes.

"Her name is Katharina; she is the poor girl who fancied she saw a ghost a fortnight ago, an apparition of doom that has since been spied by her distraught father. The poor girl has been dying ever since her first sighting of the spirit, till yesterday, when she expired."

"Tell me nothing about ghosts. I shan't sleep tonight if you do!"

"I hope there is no plague or fever coming; all this looks very like it," I continued. "The swineherd's young wife died only a week ago, and she thought something seized her by the throat as she lay in her bed, and nearly strangled her. Papa says such horrible fancies do accompany some forms of fever. She was quite well the day before. She sank afterwards and died before a week."

"Well, *her* funeral is over, I hope, and *her* hymn sung; and our ears shan't be tortured with that discord and jargon. It has made me nervous. Sit down here, beside me; sit close; hold my hand, press it hard-hard-harder."

We had moved a little back and had come to another seat.

She sat down. Her face underwent a change that alarmed and even terrified me for a moment. It darkened, and became horribly livid; her teeth and hands were clenched, and she frowned and compressed her lips, while she stared down upon the ground at her feet and trembled all over with a continued shudder as irrepressible as ague. All her energies seemed strained to suppress a fit, with which she was then breathlessly tugging; and at length a low convulsive cry of suffering broke from her, and gradually the hysteria subsided.

"There! That comes of strangling people with hymns!" she said at last. "Hold me, hold me still. It is passing away."

And so gradually it did; and perhaps to dissipate the sombre impression which the spectacle had left upon me, she became unusually animated and chatty; and so we got home.

This was the first time I had seen her exhibit any definable symptoms of that delicacy of health which her mother had spoken of. It was the first time also; I had seen her exhibit anything like temper.

Both passed away like a summer cloud; and only once afterwards did I witness on her part a momentary sign of anger. I will tell you how it happened.

She and I were looking out of one of the long drawing room windows, when there entered the courtyard, over the drawbridge, the figure of a wanderer whom I knew very well. He used to visit the schloss, generally twice a year.

It was the figure of a hunchback, with the sharp lean features that generally accompany deformity. The man's name I knew to be Aberle, and he wore a pointed black beard, and as was usual for him, was smiling from ear to ear, showing his white fangs. He was dressed in buff, black and scarlet, and crossed with more straps and belts than I could count, from which hung all manner of things. Behind, he carried a magic lantern and two boxes, which I knew well. In one there was a salamander and in the other a mandrake. These monsters used to make my father laugh. They were compounded of parts of monkeys, parrots, squirrels, fish, and hedgehogs, dried and stitched together with great neatness and startling effect. He had a fiddle, a box of conjuring apparatus, a pair of foils and masks attached to his belt, several other mysterious cases dangling about him, and a black staff with copper ferrules in his hand. His companion was a rough spare dog, which followed at his heels, but stopped short, suspiciously at the drawbridge, and in a little while began to howl dismally.

In the meantime, the mountebank, standing in the midst of the courtyard, raised his grotesque hat and made us a very ceremonious bow, paying his compliments very volubly in execrable French, and German not much better. Then, disengaging his fiddle, he began to scrape a lively air to which he sang with a merry discord, dancing with ludicrous airs and activity that made me laugh, in spite of the dog's howling.

Then he advanced to the window with many smiles and salutations, and his hat in his left hand, his fiddle under his arm, and with a fluency that never took breath, he gabbled a long advertisement of all his accomplishments and the resources of the various arts which he placed at our service, and the curiosities and entertainments which it was in his power, at our bidding, to display.

"Will your ladyships be pleased to buy an amulet against the oupire, which is going like the wolf, I hear, through these woods?" he asked, dropping his hat on the pavement. "They are dying of it right and left and here is a charm that never fails; only pinned to the pillow, and you may laugh in his face."

These charms consisted of oblong slips of vellum, with cabalistic ciphers and diagrams upon them.

Carmilla instantly expressed desire to purchase one, as did I.

Our pitchman visitor was looking up, and I was smiling down upon him, amused; at least, I can answer for myself. Carmilla though, had drawn back from the window; she pulled on the drapes just slightly, so that in part she was concealed from Aberle's view. His piercing black eye, as he looked up in our direction, seemed to be looking beyond me as though seeking a clearer view of my companion, for sure something about the girl had seemingly piqued his curiosity.

"Tell me, young lady," he laughed, "what is it about my visit that gives cause for your friend to retreat amongst the shadows? Is she perhaps so frighteningly repugnant that she feels the need to hide herself from view, during daylight hours at least, lest she should offend me with her grotesque visage?"

I gave a little giggle. I knew well enough of Aberle, to know that his words were never meant to cause offence, indeed they were at times spoken as a means of self deprecation. The man was aware that at first sight, his own form could on occasion prove quite alarming, especially for those of a most sensitive nature, hence his humour, in implying that a beautiful young woman was far more repugnant than he. I turned to Carmilla, with a smile playing across my face, a smile that quickly evaporated as I saw the scowl upon her features.

The young woman, once again, now looked very angry indeed.

"How dare that mountebank insult me so? Where is your father? I shall demand redress from him. My father would have had the wretch tied up to the pump and flogged with a cart whip, and burnt to the bones with the cattle brand!"

She retired from the window a step or two and sat down, and had hardly lost sight of the offender when her wrath subsided as suddenly as it had risen, and she gradually recovered her usual tone. I made effort to reassure her of Aberle's always good intentions, but she gestured me to be silent, and further gestured that I should leave her be.

The traveller was still in the courtyard, calling up his apologies for seemingly having overstepped his mark, and out on the drawbridge the man's dog continued to howl. Neither of these things, I decided, was conducive to improving Carmilla's spirit, and so I ventured down into the yard, where I bought two of the mountebank's amulets, one a gift for Carmilla, and the other for myself. Then I bade safe journey to both the man and his dog, before ushering them on their way.

Returning upstairs, I found that Carmilla's manner had calmed, and she seemed both excited and genuinely grateful for the charm I had bought her. She seemed oblivious to her earlier outburst regarding the little hunchback and his follies.

My father was out of spirits that evening. On coming in he told us that there had been another case very similar to the two fatal ones which had lately occurred. The sister of a young peasant on his estate, only a mile away, was very ill, and had been, as she described it, attacked very nearly in the same way, and was now slowly but steadily sinking.

"All this," said my father, "is strictly referable to natural causes. These poor people infect one another with their superstitions, and so repeat in imagination the images of terror that have infested their neighbours."

"But that very circumstance frightens one horribly," said Carmilla.

"How so?" inquired my father.

"I am so afraid of fancying I see such things; I think it would be as bad as reality."

"We are in God's hands: nothing can happen without his permission, and all will end well for those who love him. He is our faithful creator; he has made us all, and will take care of us."

"Creator? *Nature!*" said the young lady in answer to my gentle father. "And this disease that invades the country is natural. Nature, all things proceed from nature—don't they? All things in the heaven, in the earth, and under the earth, act and live as nature ordains. I think so!"

"The doctor said he would come here today," said my father, after a silence. "I want to know what he thinks about it, and what he thinks we had better do."

"Doctors never did me any good!" said Carmilla.

"Then you have been ill?" I asked.

"More ill than ever you were," she answered.

"Was it long ago?"

"Yes, a long time. I suffered from this very illness; but I forget all but my pain and weakness, and they were not as bad as are suffered in other diseases."

"You were very young then?"

"I dare say, it was long ago, but let us talk no more of it. You would not wound a friend?"

She looked languidly in my eyes, and passed her arm round my waist lovingly and led me out of the room. My father was busy over some papers near the window.

"Why does your papa like to frighten us?" asked the pretty girl, with a sigh and a little shudder.

"He doesn't, dear Carmilla. It is the very furthest thing from his mind."

"Are you afraid, dearest Laura?" she asked, wrapping her arms around my shoulders and pulling me closer to her.

"I should be very much if I fancied there was any real danger of my being attacked as those poor people were."

"You are afraid to die?" she whispered, her breath surprisingly cool against my cheek.

"Yes, everyone is."

"But to die as lovers may, to die together, so that they may live together. Girls are caterpillars while they live in the world, to be finally butterflies when the summer comes; but in the meantime there are grubs and larvae, don't you see—each with their peculiar propensities, necessities and structure. So says Monsieur Buffon, in his big book, in the next room."

Once again, her words had made little sense, but I rejoiced in the feeling of being held in those slender arms. I had no explanation for the comfort her touch brought; suffice to say, I could not imagine any future love would brighten my soul with more joy, than being around Carmilla afforded me.

Later in the day a man came, I heard him announce himself to be Dr Alvinci, and after the briefest of discussions with my papa they closeted themselves away in the study for some time. He was an exceptionally tall man, of maybe sixty years; he wore powder, and shaved his pale face as smooth as a pumpkin. When finally he and Papa emerged from the room together, I heard my father laugh and say as they came out:

"Well, I do wonder at a wise man like you. What do you say to hippogriffs and dragons?"

The doctor was smiling, and made answer, shaking his head—

"Nevertheless, life and death are mysterious states, and we know little of the resources of either."

And so they walked on, and I heard no more. I did not then know what the doctor had been broaching, but I think I guess it now.

Chapter 7

Excerpt from the journal of Doctor Alvinci. *August 11th, 1860*

It was only yesterday that I visited a number of the more affluent members of our local community, in an attempt to garner their support in easing the worries of the local peasants, and thus bringing some degree of comfort and calm to the area.

I have to confess a degree of disappointment, although not, if I am honest, total surprise, at the scepticism that greeted my assessment of the threat this region is under. Too many of these families are removed from, tucked safely away in their magnificent homes, the evil that is preying upon the peasants. I pray the fortified walls of their noble houses are thick enough to keep the devil's minions at bay.

Today though brings realisation, that whatever darkness it is that casts its shadow across these lands, evil is capable of wearing many different guises.

Today, two woodsmen, in the early hours of this morning made a most gruesome discovery, as they headed along the west road, which cuts through the forest.

It was past eight by the time they had raised the alarm, arriving panic stricken and exhausted in the nearest enclave, with shouts of "murder!" bellowing from their lungs.

It was another hour still before I arrived to inspect the scene, in order that I might give my learned assessment, regarding the remains. Several local gentry were also present, as was Father Joseph, who has been subscribed to write a report on these local disturbances, for the Imperial Commission.

I have spent many years studying medicine, and in this time I have attended the scenes of more than a few murders most foul. But there is nothing I have seen before which could in any way prepare me for the horror greeting me this morning.

This crime may well have gone unnoticed, except by chance. In this area of the forest, part of the road is lined by metre high saplings, the elder trees having been burned to blackened stumps some years earlier. A wayward bolt of lightening striking a fire which wreaked havoc on the ancient perennials, burning unrestrained for almost a week, until the heavens saw fit to check the spiteful rampage. Barely ten paces to the left of the west road, just beyond where the road takes a sharp curve away to the right, there is a clearing, and it was here that a most heinous crime was committed.

As I pushed my way past an array of sturdy saplings and entered the small clearing, which was overhung with shadows cast by the blackened remains of long dead giants. I noticed, lying on the ground at my feet, a human leg. It was almost completely bereft of flesh, except for the foot which was still partly covered by the remnants of a black boot. Deep bite marks were present along the limb at various stages, and shards of splintered bone were discarded loosely on the ground, all around.

Off to my left, two men were squatting down, inspecting the remains of what appeared to be a human arm. The hand was still attached, although a number of the fingers were missing. The heavily bloodstained limb was clothed in the vestiges of a buff material.

At the far side of the clearing, I could see another discarded limb, covered in remnants of the same buff material.

Hearing a dog growl, I turned to my right where a man was wrestling with a rather spare looking dog, of the terrier variety, which was hanging frantically to one end of a human leg. The man, who was later introduced to me as Erwin Bloch, a former gendarmerie who had moved into the vicinity from Gratz, was desperately trying to retrieve the *evidence* from the jaws of the hungry animal. It was a battle which he lost. Losing his footing, he stumbled backwards, landing with a thud onto the ground and at the same time loosing his grip on the dismembered limb. It was only a momentary slip, but still time enough for the mutt to capitalise. I shook my head disbelievingly as the small, but surprisingly powerful dog, disappeared into the foliage, its jaws clasped tightly onto its sizeable trophy, which dragged along behind the animal.

In the centre of the clearing was without doubt the oddest, not to mention most disturbing sight I have ever witnessed. On the ground, beside a burnt out campfire, there were two boxes, a fiddle, a blood stained book, and a large satchel. Beside this, buried deep into the soil, was a black staff, mounted on top of which was a severed human head. The head was that of a male, aged some thirty years plus. Many of those present recognised the victim, or at least what remained of him, as being a travelling mountebank named Aberle, who was well known throughout this vicinity.

The dead man's facial features were sharp, as was the beard that he wore. Atop his head, a pointy black hat had been repositioned, somewhat off-kilter. Dried blood stained the man's face and beard, his skin was almost marble white, the last vestiges of his body fluids having bled out onto the ground beneath the staff. His mouth drooped open and his eyes stared lifelessly across the clearing, seeing nothing, and yet saying so much. I will never forget the look of shock and horror exhibited upon that poor man's features. His face told a thousand words, and yet the crime scene left almost as many questions.

It had already been asserted, and took only minutes for me to confirm, that the wounds on the limbs were consistent with those of wolves. I say wolves, plural, because it was obvious from the differing teeth patterns displayed on the bones, we were dealing with the work of a pack of these animals, and this raises a different question. I was quickly informed by the assembled locals the presence of wolves was a scarcity within these forests and had been for some years. Rarer still were attacks upon humans, particularly at this time of year, when food within the forest is abundant. It was, however, still feasible that the animals may have attacked Aberle, especially if he had been struck down with some illness, or other malady which the beasts sensed, and thus had been left vulnerable and unable to defend himself from the animals' aggression. All of this was possible, but none of it offered any explanation as to how the dead man's severed head ended up impaled on his rod.

It was a certainty that someone else had passed the crime scene, and for reasons unknown had decided to lay out the victim's limbs around the clearing, before finally spiking the man's head upon a pole.

A thorough search of the area was carried out and the collected body parts placed into sacks, which were then placed on the back of a cart, minus, of course, the leg which the dog absconded with, and a large portion of the torso, which presumably had served as a meal for the beasts.

Aberle, I was informed by those who had known him, had been raised in a monastery in Salzburg, his parents having abandoned him due to his deformity. An end result of his time spent amongst the clergy was that he had been taught to read and write. It transpired that the book, which had been lying discarded upon the ground, was in fact a journal into which the mountebank recorded his daily musings. The dead man's possessions were placed upon the cart, although I declined placing the journal with his other belongings, opting to hold onto it, mayhap it should divulge any clue as to the events preceding his unfortunate demise.

Chapter 8

Excerpt from the journal of Aberle. *August 10th, 1860*

This has been the most fantastical day of my life; I myself find it incredulous to believe. A sale of two amulets, to the pretty young lady whose father owns the schloss overlooking the glade, had made today a success already, by my own always modest standards. However, events which have subsequently occurred go some way beyond even my wildest dreams.

I struggle to write this down; lethargy has taken a hold on my body. Something which I can only presume is a normality following the joyous rapture to which I have been exposed. And yet it was barely an hour past since I was cursing the damnable existence of a life spent sleeping under the stars. How very different I feel now.

I had built the campfire high, knowing well that the temperature would fall sharply with the onset of dusk. A peculiar mist had begun to sweep across the forest floor, making it impossible to view the ground. The damnable dog had disappeared, lost amongst the trees in pursuit of a boar, which he has little chance of catching and less chance still of subduing. Still he has not yet returned, I pray he isn't lying injured somewhere, gored on the end of angry tusks.

The fire was burning well and I had begun to doze when a figure caught my eye, moving beyond the tree line. I started, with the realisation I was not alone. Nonetheless, I called out a greeting to the stranger, extending an invitation to share the warmth from my fire. No reply was forthcoming, although a change of direction confirmed my cry had been heard. I sat motionless, intrigued as to the nature of business that had brought my guest into the forest this late in the evening. The figure approached, and although her form was obscured, concealed head to toe by a black cowl, the gracefulness with which she moved left no doubt as to her femininity; seeming almost to glide toward me, an impression further enhanced by the film of mist which advanced like smoke, obscuring her feet from my view as she approached.

"Greetings," I offered, when she came to a stop, standing over my still seated figure. "Come, warm yourself by the fire."

She did not reply.

"Pray tell, what is a fine lady such as yourself doing wandering alone at this late hour?"

"I am searching," she replied, almost in a whisper.

"For what is it that you search?"

Once again, no reply was offered, though she did push back her hood, freeing her hair and shaking it out as it fell, loosed from the restraint of the cowl. She was a young woman, maybe ten years or more my junior. Although I would say she was of above average height, she was also slight of build compared to many females her age. Her hair looked dark in the half light, and her face was very appealing, her lips curling slightly into a devilish smile, which gave her beauty an enchanting mystique.

"So what brings you---?"

She gestured me silent with a wave of her hand. Then without further intimation, she knelt beside me, and stroked her hand across my cheek, and down through my beard.

"Whatever are you doing?" I queried.

She said nothing, but planted a gentle kiss upon my face, and then pulled me toward her and kissed me hard on the mouth. So there was I, a hunchback, shorter in stature than many a child and never before having experienced so much as even the gentle caress of a woman, let alone a kiss, and now this stranger in the night was showering me with affections, with an ever increasing furore. I was lost. This could not be happening, not to me. Yet it was, and I willingly surrendered to it, with no thought of the how and why, for in truth I did not care.

The woman was kissing me with such passion it was almost impossible to catch a breath, and yet my mouth gaped open to receive her. She pushed me down onto my back, straddling me as she did so, her cloak falling open to reveal her naked body. I stared up in amazement. What was this bizarre girl doing wandering the forest at night, all but bereft of clothing? And then the thought was lost to me, as I reached out and grabbed handfuls of pert breast. I had never before so much as seen a woman unclothed, let alone had the circumstance of caressing such mounds of beauty. She was no longer kissing me; instead she was frantically tearing at my shirt, ripping open the buttons, before her hands moved lower still. I let out a small moan, feeling her hands fumbling at my crotch, and then took a sharp breath of cool night air, as finally she freed me from the restraint of my trousers. I realised what was about to happen, and I cannot lie; tears of joy welled in my eyes as she positioned herself astride me, frenetically lowering herself onto my manhood, her pelvis gyrating against my body. I closed my eyes, and bit hard into my lip. I could feel the passion rising within me, and desperately wanted this moment never to be over.

She shifted her weight, leaning forward, and once more kissing my face, before her mouth searched lower, licking and kissing my chest. I squeezed her nipples, enjoying the pliable flesh of her breasts in my hands. Knowing that for me, I was almost at the height of pleasure and would not be able to contain myself any longer. I felt the girl's mouth, nibbling at my chest hairs, and then I felt a sharp stabbing pain, like a red hot needle piercing my chest. I cried out in agony, but only for an instant. The girl's body continued to grind in sync with my own, and the peaking of my pleasure freed my mind from thoughts of all but this moment. I was lost, as a dizzying wave of delight washed over me.

It shames me to say it, but I feel the height of pleasure may have proven too much for me. It would seem that I may have fainted for some moments, for when next I opened my eyes the girl had wrapped her cloak around herself. She was standing at the edge of the clearing, looking away from me. I called to her that she should stay and that I did not even know her name. She looked back just once, and then in the instant in which it took me to blink my eyes she was gone, leaving the rather unfortunate sight of this dishevelled dwarf, with breeches dropped around my ankles, lying exhausted beside the burning campfire. The fire's glow, flickering eerily against the backdrop of the transparent veil of creeping fog, served only to add to the absurdity of the situation in which I now found myself.

I write a record of these events down now, even though the languidness that sweeps through me makes doing so difficult in the extreme. Nonetheless, it is important I make note of this, so that in the morning when I awaken, I am not led to believe that the whole episode was but a night fantasy. Indeed it was not, and as ever long as it may take me to do so, I shall find this girl again. Doubtless, she is highly unlikely to be found wanting of male attention, and is even less likely to desire an unfortunate such as I be her suitor. She has shown me a great kindness, and granted me an experience for which I shall be forever grateful. As such I must tell her so, indebted to her as I will always be.

As joyful as this night has been, a strange melancholy continues to stir within me. Maybe I am just worrying about my four legged companion, it has been some hours now and still he has not returned.

I feel so devoid of energy I can barely move, I had not realised lovemaking was such a strenuous occurrence. I will sleep now, and if Dog has not returned by daybreak then I shall venture forth in search of him.

This is a most worrying situation. I don't know for how long I have slept, although judged on the way the fire has burnt down I would guess no more than a couple of hours.

I was awakened with a start, by the howling of wolves, at a distance that is far too close to be deemed acceptable. I am still languid, but luckily had already stocked up on firewood for the night.

They have moved in closer now. Even through the mist which has thickened, I can see them moving amongst the saplings, and they are mighty beasts. They seem far larger, in fact, than any wolves I have ever previously seen. Thankfully, the flames from the fire will be enough to keep them at bay.

There is a mystery developing here, and it is one that is most frightful. A short while ago, a huge black wolf broke away from the rest of the pack and moved steadily out from the tree line approaching up to where I stood, stopping just a few metres short of my position. By this time I had lit a torch and was waving it before me, but the animal seemed disinterested and unafraid of the flames. The wolf stood watching me and sniffed the air intently, before slowly turning away and heading back towards the other creatures. It is a worry that this beast does not fear flame, even more so if his kin are equally fearless.

I know now that evil is afoot this night. My vigour still deserts me, and worse, the wolves are still moving beyond the tree line; agitatedly so, as if waiting for something.

I could not be sure that my eyes weren't playing tricks on me in the dark, but on more than a few occasions I believed I glimpsed men moving amongst the trees too. I feared calling out to them, lest it did spark the beasts into attacking me. Now though, I fear my problems are greater than first suspected. I glimpsed just once the figure of a naked man, standing beyond the burned out oak, on the south side of the clearing. Our eyes met, if only for the briefest of moments, when suddenly he dropped onto all fours, his body contorting as he did so, and when this fiend again looked upon me, it was through the yellow eyes of a wolf.

It will be daylight in a couple of hours; pray the Lord keeps me safe until then. I doubt such hell fiends as these will attack once the sun rises. Pray the Lord God protects me.

Chapter 9

Correspondence from Laura Bennett, addressed to Doctor Hesselius. *March 20th, 1871*

There called one evening, not long after Carmilla had joined our happy group, the dark-faced son of the picture cleaner. He arrived from Gratz, with a horse and cart laden with two large packing cases, having many pictures in each. It was a journey of ten leagues, and whenever a messenger arrived at the schloss from our little capital of Gratz, we used to crowd about him in the hall to hear the news.

This arrival created in our secluded quarters quite a sensation. The cases remained in the hall, and the messenger was taken charge of by the servants till he had eaten his supper. Then, with assistants, and armed with hammer, ripping chisel, and turn-screw, he met us in the hall, where we had assembled to witness the unpacking of the cases.

Carmilla sat looking listlessly on, while one after the other the old pictures, nearly all portraits which had undergone the process of renovation, were brought to light. My mother was of an old

Hungarian family, and most of these pictures, which were about to be restored to their places, had come to us through her.

My father had a list in his hand from which he read, as the artist rummaged out the corresponding numbers. I don't know that the pictures were very good, but they were undoubtedly very old and some of them very curious also. They had for the most part the merit of being now seen by me, I may say for the first time, for the smoke and dust of time had all but obliterated them.

"There is a picture that I have not seen yet," said my father. "In one corner at the top of it, is the name as well as I could read, 'Marcia Karnstein,' and the date '1698'; and I remain curious to see how it has turned out."

I remembered it; it was a small picture, about a foot and a half high and nearly square, without a frame, but it was so blackened by age that I could not make it out.

The artist now produced it, with evident pride. It was quite beautiful; it was startling how it seemed so alive. It was the effigy of Carmilla!

"Carmilla, dear, here is an absolute miracle. Here you are, living, smiling, and ready to speak, in this picture. Isn't it beautiful, Papa? And see, even the little mole on her throat."

My father laughed, and said "Certainly it is a wonderful likeness," but he looked away, and to my surprise seemed but little struck by it, and went on talking to the picture cleaner, who was also something of an artist, and discoursed with intelligence about the portraits or other works which his art had just brought into light and colour, while I was more and more lost in wonder the more I looked at the picture.

"Will you let me hang this picture in my room, Papa?" I asked.

"Certainly, dear," said he, smiling, "I'm very glad you think it so alike. It must be prettier even than I thought it, if it is."

The young lady did not acknowledge this pretty speech, did not seem to hear it. She was leaning back in her seat, her fine eyes under their long lashes gazing on me in contemplation, and she smiled in a kind of rapture.

"And now, Papa, you can read quite plainly the name that is written in the corner. It is not Marcia; it looks as if it was done in gold. The name is Mircalla, Countess Karnstein, and this is a little coronet over and underneath A.D. 1698. I am descended from the Karnsteins; that is, Mamma was."

"Ah!" said the lady, listlessly, "so am I, I think a very long descent, very ancient. Are there any Karnsteins living now?"

"None who bear the name, I believe. The family were ruined, I believe in some civil wars long ago, but the ruins of the castle are only about three miles away."

"How interesting!" she said, languidly. "But see what beautiful moonlight!"

She glanced through the hall door, which stood a little open. "Might you take a little ramble round the court, and look down at the road and river."

"It is so like the night you came to us," I reflected.

She sighed; smiling. She rose, and with our arms round each other's waist, we walked out upon the pavement. In silence, slowly we walked down to the drawbridge, where the beautiful landscape opened before us.

"And so you were thinking of the night I came here?" she repeated, almost in a whisper. "Are you glad I came?"

"Delighted, dearest Carmilla," I answered.

"And you asked for the picture you think like me, to hang in your room," she murmured with a sigh, as she drew her arm closer about my waist, and let her pretty head sink upon my shoulder.

"How romantic you are, Carmilla," I said. "Whenever you tell me your story, it will be made up chiefly of some one great romance."

She kissed my cheek, silently.

"I am sure, Carmilla, you have been in love; that there is at this moment, an affair of the heart going on."

"I have been in love with no one, and never shall," she whispered, "unless it should be with you."

How beautiful she looked in the moonlight!

Shy and strange was the look with which she quickly hid her face in my neck and hair, with tumultuous sighs, that seemed almost to sob, and pressed in mine a hand that trembled. Her soft cheek was glowing against mine, and I felt again that strangest of aches in the pit of my stomach, for something of which I knew not.

"Darling, darling," she murmured, "I live in you; and you would die for me, I love you so."

I started from her, alarmed by her talk of dying.

She was gazing on me with eyes from which all fire, all meaning had flown, and a face colourless and apathetic.

"Is there a chill in the air, dear?" she said drowsily. "I almost shiver; have I been dreaming? Let us come in. Come; come; come in."

"You look ill, Carmilla; a little faint. You certainly must take some wine," I said, as I ushered my companion back towards the schloss.

"Yes. I will. I'm better now. I shall be quite well in a few minutes. Yes, do give me a little wine," answered Carmilla, as we approached the door. "Let us look again for a moment; it is the last time perhaps, I shall see the moonlight with you."

Doubtless, my face had registered the concern I felt at her strange statement.

"Worry not for me, darling Laura," she pleaded. "There are far greater concerns to be lauded over in life, than to fret over one such as I."

"My dearest Carmilla, how could I ever not worry about your well being?" I asked. "Mere moments ago, you stated that you 'love me so.' I truly had not realised, until you spoke thus, but for certain you hold a place within my heart. I cannot claim to fully understand the emotions you raise within me; all I know is that to have you in my life, fills me with gaiety."

Carmilla smiled, and gently squeezed my waist. "Come, darling; let us partake of some wine now. For truly that, along with your kind words will surely lift my spirit."

"How do you feel now, dear Carmilla? Are you really better?" I asked, as I passed her a goblet of our finest red. I was beginning to take alarm, lest she should have been stricken with the strange epidemic that they said had invaded the country about us.

"Papa would be grieved beyond measure," I added, "if he thought you were ever so little ill, without immediately letting us know. We have a doctor near us, the physician who was with Papa today. He is new to our district, but word among the servants is that he is a very skilful man."

"I'm sure he is. I know how kind you all are, but dear child, I am quite well again. There is nothing ever wrong with me, but a little weakness. People say I am languid; I am incapable of exertion; I can scarcely walk as far as a child of three years old. Every now and then the little strength I have falters and I become as you have just seen me. But after all I am very easily set up again; in a moment I am perfectly myself. See how I have recovered?"

So indeed she had. She and I talked a great deal and very animated she was, but the remainder of that evening passed without any recurrence of what I called her infatuations. I mean her crazy talk of dying, which, if I am to be honest, had perturbed and frightened me. But there occurred later that night, an event which gave my thoughts quite a new turn. I have never since discussed what happened on that night with anyone, but I think it necessary now to set things down for you, in order that you might fully understand the nature of what was occurring. I can only trust that you do not judge me too harshly…

Chapter 10

Correspondence from Laura Bennett, addressed to Doctor Hesselius. *March 20th, 1871*

We were seated in the drawing room, and having finished partaking of some wine, we chatted gaily as young women often do.

Carmilla's mood had lightened, possibly as a result of finishing her second glass, and she joyfully questioned me about all aspects of my childhood in Styria. Mademoiselle De Lafontaine later joined us and delighted with stories of her experiences whilst teaching in the Far East. The Land of the Rising Sun sounded a most fascinating place indeed.

As the evening wore on, Mademoiselle De Lafontaine passed comment on the pallor that had washed over Carmilla's features. I explained about her suffering a most peculiar turn whilst we had been out walking, which had worried me greatly. Carmilla made light of this and attempted to laugh off the worries of Mademoiselle De Lafontaine and myself, putting both her 'pallor' and her 'peculiar turn' down to not having slept well the previous night.

It was suggested by Mademoiselle De Lafontaine, that a warm bath before bed may help to lift Carmilla's spirits, and she instructed two of the servants to place our largest tub beside the hearth in Carmilla's room, the fire already having been struck. Whilst the servants were drawing the water, the three of us enjoyed coffee and chocolate.

Having bid a good night to Mademoiselle De Lafontaine, I accompanied Carmilla to her room and sat idly chatting to her whilst the servants finished topping up the bath with hot water, and laying out jugs of rinsing water onto the hearth.

Carmilla ran her hand over the bundle of soft white towels, which had been placed upon the bed.

"Dear Laura, pray that I might ask of you a favour?"

"A favour? Of course, you should know that you can ask anything of me, and wherever it is possible I would indulge you."

"Then stay with me for a while. I still, if I am honest, do not feel filled with vigour, and worry about becoming faint whilst cleansing myself. Yet I have no desire to bathe under the gaze of a servant. I would much rather have you sitting with me, my love."

Now if I am to be honest, I felt somewhat strange at the prospect of seeing Carmilla disrobed. Not uncomfortable, more a slight knotting within the pit of my stomach and an increased pressure within my chest, as though my heart was beating more powerfully than normal.

Carmilla, I guessed, sensed some reserve tugging at my soul, or maybe it was just my reluctance to instantly give consent to her request. Either way, she smiled and gently squeezed my hand in hers, and my resolve melted.

"Very well," I obliged.

She let out a girlish squeal of excitement as I yielded to her desire, then instantly set about ordering the servants to hurry in completing their tasks, so they might sooner vacate the room with orders not to return until the morning.

Once the room was emptied, save for the two of us, Carmilla turned her back on me, and asked that I unbutton her as she wanted to take her bath whilst the water was still nicely warm. I undid the clasp on her dress and then turned away, intent on averting my gaze until she was fully immersed in the bathtub. I did not turn back around until after I had heard the splash of Carmilla lowering herself into the water.

I then pulled up a chair, placing it alongside the tub, although of course I was positioned higher than Carmilla, who was all but submerged up to her shoulders in the still steaming bath. It astonished me that she was able to cope so readily with the heat of the water, its vapour causing my face to redden and dampen.

Carmilla gave the slightest of giggles, "Darling Laura, how your skin does glow, it seems almost to shimmer with the beauty of your exquisite features."

I shook my head. How this girl could talk of my beauty, when she laid there, her body all but submerged, except for one finely shaped knee extended above the waterline, her foot pressed firm to the tubs base.

"Dearest Carmilla," I smiled, "how is it that you can talk of my beauty, do you not realise you are surely the fairest maiden ever to grace the halls of this humble schloss?"

She laughed out loud. "Dearest, your words flatter me. But rest assured if you truly find me to be a creature of beauty, it is for sure no more bewitching than the way in which my own eyes regard you."

I stroked gentle fingers through her hair. "Dear Carmilla, I shall be eternally grateful that the fates chose to bring us together."

"As am I, my dear. Now come, will you not consider joining me?"

"What?" I started, unsure as to whether I had misheard her proposal.

"Your face glows with perspiration, for this is truly the hottest bath I have ever taken, and combined with the roaring of the fire for certain you cannot find comfort in your apparel. Join me, sweet Laura, so we might splash as children playfully wading in the duck pond."

"I think I should not, for it would not be right!"

"Have we not, us two, been thrown together by fate? Did we not meet in our dreams when we were but small children? I love you so, dear Laura, as you too love me. Do not be afraid to take hold of my hand and join me."

Thinking back now, I know this did not seem right, as I knew then that it was not right. As always though, with Carmilla, it was all but impossible for me to resist her charms, and truthfully, the idea of the warm water washing over me as I chatted to my beloved, it was a speculation I found most appealing.

I insisted that Carmilla cover her eyes whilst I disrobed. Discarding my attire over the back of the chair I had been sitting on, I stepped with a certain delicacy into the warm water. Carmilla was lying, eyes closed, with her neck resting over the back of the tub. Facing my back to her; I slid my body below the surface line, gently prising her legs apart as I did so in order to make a seat for myself. She giggled loudly, as with a 'plinking' sound; my bottom thumped against the base of the bathtub.

The warm water at once began to ease the tensions within my body. I felt my muscles loosen and grow slack. Without any word, Carmilla began softly splashing water across my back, and then she gently soaped me, before moving on to running her fingers across my damp skin. This produced a squeaking sound, as her slender digits pressed the soapy water across my bare flesh, and we both began laughing inanely. She continued caressing me and I relaxed further, every nerve in my body becoming quiet, my brain dull, almost numb, as Carmilla tenderly massaged my neck and shoulders.

"My turn now," she said, abruptly, but with a playful giggle. Lifting her left leg clear of the water, her knee positioned just in front of my face.

I gave a sigh, she had almost sent me to heaven, and I hadn't wanted her sweet caress to end. It was only fair though that I should indulge her too. Picking up the soap, I began washing her slender but shapely leg. I marvelled at the softness of her flesh, the contours of this beautiful limb which I held in my hands. I traced my fingers across her skin, stroking gently every inch of that fine leg, down as far as her ankles, then back again, until I found myself kneading her soft thigh. She let out a little moan, and I knew then that I should stop, but I continued, until finally Carmilla pulled my hands away.

"Stand up," she whispered, "we should rinse off with fresh water."

I was disappointed that she had so soon chosen to end our mutual bathing, but also worried that she felt I had overstepped the mark in some way. Carmilla stood up, her fine slender form looking more magnificent than I might ever have believed possible. With surprisingly strong hands she helped me erect and held me to prevent me from slipping. Then, with no thought of rinsing ourselves down, Carmilla once again began soaping my body. I was shocked but also enthralled by the provocative nature of her actions, hands fluttering across my belly, tracing tiny circles across my skin, fingers moving higher and lower, easing and exploring every mound and hollow. I sighed loudly and told myself I should protest. But I did nothing. And when she moved closer to me, our bodies pressed together thigh to thigh, torso to torso, and her head moving down to kiss me, not as a friend but as a lover, I returned in kind.

I am not quite sure how, but we ended on the bed, skin on skin, body pressed on body, stroking, caressing, twisting and turning, building gradually to that final moment for which I had no name. Although I have since learned that it was on this night, I first experienced la petite mort.

Chapter 11

Correspondence from Laura Bennett, addressed to Doctor Hesselius. *March 22nd, 1871*

I am still unsure that I should have included certain information, pertaining to events of a private and sensitive nature, in my recent correspondence with your good self. I can only pray that you do not see fit to judge me too harshly for the sinner I am; however, I do feel it necessary to tell all, in the hope that you may fully understand the powerful nature of the love that we two shared. Also, I feel it best to keep nothing from you, insofar that you might gain a true and accurate account regarding the turn of events, which happened those years ago.

My sleep that night can best be described as fitful, dreams of a certain nature, and regarding Carmilla, filled my every sleeping moment. When I awoke in the early hours; the candles had burned down, as had the fire, leaving the room in semi-darkness. I was aware of a lack of vigour running through me, possibly, I surmised, due to the glorious exertions of the previous hours. Carmilla's naked body was curled into mine, her soft warm breath playing on the back of my neck. I gently released myself from her embrace, and silently slipped off the bed, being equally stealthy as I climbed back into my clothes. I placed the gentlest of kisses on my lover's forehead, before creeping out of the door and along the landing, towards the sanctity of my bedroom.

I did not rise early the next day, but was still up some hours before Carmilla.

I was disappointed when Madame Perrodon informed me that Papa had been called away, to deal with some urgent matters of business, and that he was unlikely to return much before nightfall.

I spent much of the morning sitting alone in the drawing room, as I felt decidedly melancholy. Although I put this down to worrying about the events of the previous night, concerned as I was to how Carmilla might now perceive our friendship. I had my reservations over that which had occurred, although the thoughts of it also excited me greatly. However, I had no wish to estrange or cause upset to Carmilla, and hoped that her actions had not been swayed by the wine we had drank.

It was past two in the afternoon when Carmilla finally surfaced, a late rising even by her standards. I should not have worried about which type of presentation to expect from her, she appeared positively radiant and her form showed vigour of movement unparalleled during her time with us.

Both Madame Perrodon and Mademoiselle De Lafontaine, passed comment as to how well Carmilla appeared. She in turn remarked that, 'A sound night's rest had done her the world of good.' Both ladies also noted how I appeared particularly drawn, with a certain pallor affecting my skin. In truth, I was worrying about repercussions from the previous evening. I was not sure that Papa, although considered a liberal man, would understand such behaviour should it ever come to light.

It was late in the afternoon before I finally managed to find time alone with Carmilla. I attempted to tell her of my worries, and to seek reassurance from her, but she just laughed off my concerns. She placed her arm around my waist, and pulling me close, whispered, "If ever but once I loved, then surely that love is you. I would never hurt you, my darling, no more than any one lover ever hurts another."

I so wished the girl would desist from talking in riddles!

Although I did at least understand enough of it to realise she too had been enthralled by our night together, and was most unlikely to make common knowledge of our liaison.

It was past seven in the evening when Papa finally arrived home. We had not long moved into the drawing room, having just sat down to partake of our coffee and chocolate, although Carmilla did not take any. Madame and Mademoiselle De Lafontaine had joined us; we were in the process of making a little card party, when Papa made his entrance.

His face was drawn, and he looked most troubled, although he denied our requests to unburden him.

All he would say was, "It has been a most horrible day, I have learned much which troubles me, but it is not the sort of thing to burden ladies such as you with. God willing, whatever wretched thing it is afflicting this region, soon a combination of the finest medical minds and the Lords good grace, will see fit to banish this pestilence from these lands."

Papa bid us to continue with our card party, and then called for a servant to fetch him what he called his "dish of tea."

He bid us continue our game and watched silently as we played the first few hands. Papa continued to steadily sip at his tea, and although his eyes were upon us, it was obvious to all that he was distracted. Once finished, he instructed a servant that he would be in the dining room in ten minutes, so to make ready his meal. He then swiftly departed from us, in order to change into more comfortable attire before partaking of his supper.

Our card party lasted a few hours, so by the time we finished Papa had rejoined us. After the game was over, he sat down beside Carmilla on the sofa, and asked her a little anxiously, whether she had heard from her mother since her arrival.

She answered, "No."

He then asked whether she knew where a letter would reach her at present.

"I cannot tell," she answered ambiguously, "but I have been thinking of leaving you; you have been already too hospitable and too kind to me. I have given you an infinity of trouble, I should wish to take a carriage tomorrow and post in pursuit of her; I know where I shall ultimately find her, although I dare not yet tell you!"

I must admit to having been both horrified and almost struck dumb by Carmilla's declaration. Maybe our previous intimacy had presented far more implications than I first realised.

"But you must not dream of any such thing," exclaimed my father, to my great relief. "We can't afford to lose you so, and I won't consent to your leaving us, except under the care of your mother; who was so good as to allow you to remain with us till she herself returns. I should be quite happy if I knew that you heard from her: but this day, while I have no wish to place the weight of things learned upon you, nevertheless, the accounts of the progress of the mysterious disease which has invaded our neighbourhood grows ever more alarming. My beautiful guest, I do feel the responsibility unaided by advice from your mother very much. But I shall do my best and one thing is certain, that you must not think of leaving us without her distinct direction to this effect. We should suffer too much in parting from you to consent to it easily."

"Thank you, sir, a thousand times for your hospitality," she answered, smiling bashfully. "You have all been too kind to me; I have seldom been so happy in all my life before, as in your beautiful schloss, under your care, and in the society of your dear daughter."

So he gallantly, in his old-fashioned way kissed her hand, smiling and pleased at her little speech. For my part I was more than pleased to hear her affirm that her fondness for me remained.

It was growing late, so I accompanied Carmilla to her room, then sat and chatted with her while she was preparing for bed.

"Do you think," I said at length, "that you will ever confide fully in me?"

She turned around smiling, but made no answer, only continued to smile on me.

"You won't answer that?" I said. "You can't answer pleasantly; I ought not to have asked you!"

"You were quite right to ask me that, or anything. For surely you know how dear you are to me, or you could not think any confidence too great to look for. Surely our love cannot be in any doubt to you? But know this, I am under vows and I dare not tell my story yet, even to you. The time is very near when you shall know everything. You will think me cruel, very selfish, but love is always selfish; the more ardent the more selfish. How jealous I am you cannot know. You must come with me, loving me, to death; or else hate me and still come with me, *hating* me through death and after. There is no such word as indifference in my apathetic nature."

"Now, Carmilla, you are going to talk your wild nonsense again," I said hastily.

"Not I, silly little fool as I am, and full of whims and fancies; for your sake I'll talk like a sage. Were you ever at a ball?"

"No, I never was; how you do run on so. What is it like? How charming it must be," I asked, eagerly, captivated by the girl's whimsical digress.

"I almost forget, it is years ago."

I laughed.

"You are not so old. Your first ball can hardly be forgotten yet!"

"I remember everything about it—with an effort. I see it all, as one who dives beneath the water can see what is going on above, through a medium, dense, rippling, but transparent. There occurred that night what has confused the picture and made its colours faint. I was all but assassinated in my bed, wounded here," she touched her breast, "and never was the same since."

"Were you near dying?"

"Yes, very—a cruel love—a strange love, that would have taken my life. Love will have its sacrifices. No sacrifice without blood. Let us go to sleep now; I feel so lazy. How can I get up just now and lock my door?"

She was lying with her tiny hands buried in her rich wavy hair, under her cheek, her little head upon the pillow, and her glittering eyes followed me wherever I moved, with a kind of shy smile that I could not decipher.

"I could stay awhile," I offered.

"No," she cut me short. "Do not fear, my darling, we shall have our time. But not tonight, for my vigour fails me now and most assuredly I must rest."

I confess to having felt a little disappointed, hurt almost, at what I took to be her rather brusque dispatching of my person. Nonetheless I hid my feelings, bid her good night, and crept from the room with an uncomfortable sadness clawing at my soul.

I often wondered whether our pretty guest ever said her prayers. I certainly had never seen her upon her knees. In the morning she never came down until long after our family prayers were over, and at night she never left the drawing room to attend our brief evening prayers in the hall.

If it had not been that it had casually come out in one of our careless talks that she had been baptised, I should have doubted her being a Christian. After all, Religion was a subject on which I had barely heard her speak a word. If I had known the world better, this particular neglect or antipathy would not have so much surprised me.

The precautions of nervous people are infectious, and persons of a like temperament are pretty sure, after a time, to imitate them. I had adopted Carmilla's habit of locking her bedroom door, having taken into my head all her whimsical alarms about midnight invaders and prowling assassins. I had also adopted her precaution of making a brief search through her room, to satisfy herself that no lurking assassin or robber was "ensconced."

These wise measures taken, I got into my bed and fell asleep. A light was burning in my room. This was an old habit of very early date, and which nothing could have tempted me to dispense with.

Thus fortified I might take my rest in peace. But dreams come through stone walls, light up dark rooms or darken light ones, and their persons make their exits and their entrances as they please, laughing at locksmiths.

I had a dream that night that was the beginning of a very strange agony.

I cannot call it a nightmare, for I was quite conscious of being asleep. But I was equally conscious of being in my room, lying in bed precisely as I actually was. I saw, or fancied I saw, the room and its furniture just as I had seen it last, except that it was very dark, and I saw something moving round the foot of the bed, which at first I could not accurately distinguish. But I soon saw it was a sooty-black animal resembling a monstrous cat. It appeared to me about four or five feet long, for it measured fully the length of the hearthrug as it passed over it; and it continued toing and froing with the lithe, sinister restlessness of a caged beast. I could not cry out, although as you may suppose, I was terrified. Its pace was growing faster, and the room rapidly darker and darker, and at length so dark that I could no longer see anything of it but its eyes. I felt it spring lightly on the bed. The two broad eyes approached my face, and I closed my eyes in panic. Fear held me rigid, as the acrid breath of the creature played over my throat. Suddenly I felt a stinging pain as if two large needles darted, an inch or two apart, deep into my breast. I awoke with a scream. The room was lighted by the candle that burnt there all through the night, and I saw a female figure standing at the foot of the bed, a little at the right side. It was in a dark loose riding hood, which seemed to shimmer and move as though imbedded with a will of its own. The apparition's hair was down and fell forward from the cowl, covering her shoulders. A block of stone could not have been more still. There was not the slightest stir of respiration. As I stared at it the figure appeared to have changed its place, and was now nearer the door; then close to it, the door opened, and it passed out.

I was now relieved, and able to breathe and move. My first thought was that Carmilla had been playing a trick on me and that I had forgotten to secure my door. I hastened to it and found it locked as usual on the inside. I was afraid to open it—I was horrified. I sprang into my bed and covered my head up in the bedclothes, and lay there more dead than alive till morning.

Chapter 12

A letter written by Baron Vordenburg, addressed to Doctor Alvinci. Dated *August 17th, 1860*

Dear Doctor Alvinci,

I was both intrigued and alarmed in equal measures upon receipt of your letter regarding the affliction which is plaguing your district. A recent communiqué from an old friend had already alerted me to the possibility of such an outbreak.

I do remember our previous conversation, at the home of Baroness von Waxensteini, and can garner enough from our first meeting to know that you are a man of substance, thus unlikely to be easily swayed by the histrionics of the laity.

It has been my misfortune to have had dealings with various types of pernicious evil, certainly some of which compare behaviourally to the ills which you yourself now face. The good news is, I am more than confident that I can help you to dispatch this evil, indeed I already have my suspicions where the root of this problem is quite possibly to be found.

My last sentence may come as something of a surprise to you, but forgive me if I choose not to elaborate on it at this time.

Suffice to say, this matter is receiving my full and immediate attention. I intend to head into Gratz at break of day tomorrow, as there are a number of recorded documents which I need to search through, as I believe the answer to your dilemma lays both in antiquity, and, indeed, close to home. Rest assured I shall dispatch word to you of the actions that need to be undertaken, as soon as I am able.

Sincerely yours,

Baron Vordenburg

Chapter 13

Correspondence from Laura Bennett, addressed to Doctor Hesselius. *March 22nd, 1871*

It would be completely in vain, my attempting to tell you the full horror with which, even now, I recall the occurrence of that previous night's happening, which I have described to you. It was no such transitory terror as a dream leaves behind it. It seemed to deepen by time and communicated itself to the room and the very furniture that had encompassed the apparition.

I could not bear next day to be alone for a moment. I should have told Papa, but for two opposing reasons. At one time I thought he would laugh at my story, and I could not bear its being treated as a jest; and at another I thought he might fancy I had been attacked by the mysterious complaint which had invaded our neighbourhood. I myself had no misgiving of the kind, and as he had been rather an invalid for some time, I was afraid of alarming him.

I was comfortable enough with my good-natured companions, Madame Perrodon, and Mademoiselle Lafontaine. They both perceived me to be out of spirits and nervous, and at length I told them what lay so heavy at my heart.

Mademoiselle laughed, but I fancied Madame Perrodon looked anxious.

"By-the-by," said Mademoiselle, laughing, "The long lime tree walk, behind Carmilla's bedroom window, is haunted!"

"Nonsense!" exclaimed Madame, who probably thought the theme rather inopportune, "and who tells that story, my dear?"

"Martin says that he came up twice when the old yard gate was being repaired, just before sunrise, and twice saw the same female figure walking down the lime tree avenue."

"So he well might, as long as there are cows to milk in the river field," said Madame.

"I daresay; but Martin chooses to be frightened, and never did I see a fool more frightened."

"You must not say a word about it to Carmilla, because she can see down that walk from her window," I interposed, "and she is if possible, a greater coward than I."

Carmilla came down rather later than usual that day.

"I was so frightened last night," she said, as soon as we were together, "and I am sure I should have seen something dreadful if it had not been for that charm you bought from the poor little hunchback whom I called such harsh names. I had a dream of something black coming around my bed, and I awoke in a perfect horror. I really thought, for some seconds, I saw a dark figure near the chimney-piece, but I felt under my pillow for my charm, and the moment my fingers touched it the figure disappeared. I felt quite certain, only that I had it by me, that something frightful would have made its appearance and perhaps throttled me, as it did those poor people we heard of."

"Well, listen to me," I began, and recounted my adventure, at the recital of which she appeared horrified.

"And had you the charm near you?" she asked, earnestly.

"No, I had dropped it into a china vase in the drawing room, but I shall certainly take it with me tonight, as you have so much faith in it."

At this distance of time I cannot tell you, or even understand how I overcame my horror so effectually as to lie alone in my room that night. I remember distinctly that I pinned the charm to my pillow. I fell asleep almost immediately and slept even more soundly than usual all night.

Next night I passed as well. My sleep was delightfully deep and dreamless. But I wakened with a sense of lassitude and melancholy, which, however, did not exceed a degree that was almost luxurious.

"Well I told you so," said Carmilla, when I described my quiet sleep. "I had such delightful sleep myself last night; I pinned the charm to the breast of my nightdress, it was too far away the night before. I am quite sure it was all but fantasy, except the dreams. I used to think that evil spirits made dreams, but our doctor told me it is no such thing. It is merely a fever passing by, or some other malady, as they often do. He said it comes knocking at the door of our psyche, and not being able to get in, passes on, its touch laying a fright upon us as it does so."

"Then what do you think the charm is?" said I.

"It has been fumigated or immersed in some drug, and is an antidote against the malaria," she answered.

"Then it acts only on the body?"

"On the body and on the mind, certainly; you don't suppose evil spirits are frightened by bits of ribbon, or the perfumes of a druggist's shop? No, these complaints, wandering in the air, begin by trying the nerves, and so infect the brain; but before they can seize upon you the antidote repels them. This, I am sure, is what the charm has done for us. It is nothing magical, it is simply natural."

I should have been happier if I could have quite agreed with Carmilla, but I did my best, and the impression was a little losing its force.

For some nights I slept soundly; but still every morning I felt the same lassitude, and a languor weighed upon me all day. I felt myself a changed girl. A strange melancholy was stealing over me, a melancholy I would not have interrupted. Dim thoughts of death began to open; ideas that I was slowly sinking took a gentle and somehow not unwelcome possession of me. If it was sad, the tone of mind which this induced was also sweet. Whatever it might be my soul acquiesced in it.

I would not admit that I was ill; I would not consent to tell Papa, or to have the doctor sent for.

Carmilla became more devoted to me than ever, and her strange paroxysms of languid adoration more frequent. She applied herself to me with increasing ardour, showering me in passionate kisses, and gentle caresses, all the more as my strength and spirits waned. This always shocked me like a momentary glare of insanity on her part, as though she seemed oblivious as to how depleted of vitality I was becoming.

Without knowing it, I was now in an advanced stage of the strangest illness under which a mortal can ever suffer. There was an unaccountable fascination in its earlier symptoms that more than reconciled me to the incapacitating effect of that stage of the malady. This fascination increased for a time until it reached a certain point, when gradually a sense of the horrible mingled itself with it, deepening as you shall hear, until it discoloured and perverted the whole state of my life.

The first change I experienced was rather agreeable. It was very near the turning point from which began my descent into the darkest depths of Avernus.

Certain vague and strange sensations visited me in my sleep. The prevailing one was of that pleasant, peculiar cold thrill which we feel in bathing, when we move against the current of a river. This was soon accompanied by dreams that seemed interminable, and were so vague I could never recollect their scenery and persons, or any one connected portion of their action. But they left an awful impression and a sense of exhaustion, as if I had passed through a long period of great mental exertion and danger.

After all these dreams, there remained on waking a remembrance of having been in a place very nearly dark. Of having spoken to people whom I could not see; especially of one clear voice, of a female's, very deep, that spoke as if at a distance, slowly, and producing always the same sensation of an indescribable solemnity and fear. Sometimes there came a sensation as if a hand was drawn softly along my cheek and neck. Sometimes it was as if warm lips kissed the whole of me, tenderly, longer and longer and ever more lovingly as they reached my throat, but there the caress fixed itself. My heart beat faster, my breathing rose and fell rapidly and full drawn; a sobbing, crying, that began with feelings of joy, akin to those I had experienced together with Carmilla, but rose into a sense of strangulation, supervened and turned into a dreadful convulsion, in which my senses left me and I became unconscious.

It was now three weeks since the commencement of this unaccountable state. My sufferings had, during the last week, told upon my appearance. I had grown pale, my eyes were dilated and darkened underneath, and the languor which I had long felt began to display itself in my countenance.

My father asked me often whether I was ill; but, with an obstinacy which now seems to me unaccountable, I persisted in assuring him that I was quite well.

In a sense this was true. I had no pain, I could complain of no bodily derangement. My complaint seemed to be one of the imagination or the nerves, horrible as my sufferings were, I kept them, with a morbid reserve, very nearly to myself.

It could not be that terrible complaint which the peasants called the oupire, for I had now been suffering for three weeks and they were seldom ill for much more than three days, before death put an end to their miseries.

Carmilla complained of dreams and feverish sensations, but by no means of so alarming a kind as mine. I say that mine were extremely alarming. Had I been capable of comprehending my condition, I would have invoked aid and advice on my knees. The narcotic of an unsuspected influence was acting upon me, and my perceptions were benumbed.

I am going to tell you now of a dream which led immediately to an odd discovery. One night, instead of the voice I was accustomed to hear in the dark, I heard one sweet and tender, and at the same time terrible, which said, "Your mother warns you to beware of the assassin." At the same time a light unexpectedly sprang up, and I saw Carmilla standing near the foot of my bed, in her white nightdress, bathed from her chin to her feet in one great stain of blood.

I wakened with a shriek, possessed with the one idea that Carmilla was being murdered. I remember springing from my bed, and my next recollection is one of standing in the lobby, crying for help.

Madame and Mademoiselle came scurrying out of their rooms in alarm; a lamp burned always in the lobby, and seeing me, they soon learned the cause of my terror.

I insisted on our knocking at Carmilla's door. Our knocking was unanswered. It soon became a pounding and soon progressed to uproar. We shrieked her name, but all was in vain.

We all grew frightened, for the door was locked. We hurried back in panic to my room. There we rang the bell long and furiously. If my father's room had been at that side of the house, we would have called him up at once to our aid. But, alas! He was quite out of hearing, and to reach him involved an excursion for which we none of us had courage.

Servants however, soon came running up the stairs. I had got on my dressing gown and slippers meanwhile, and my companions were already similarly furnished. Recognizing the voices of the servants in the lobby, we sallied out together; and having renewed, as fruitlessly, our summons at Carmilla's door, I ordered the men to force the lock. They did so, and we stood holding our lights aloft, in the doorway, and so stared into the room.

We called her by name; but there was still no reply. We looked round the room. Everything was undisturbed. It was exactly in the state in which I had left it on bidding her goodnight. But Carmilla was gone.

Chapter 14

Correspondence from Laura Bennett, addressed to Doctor Hesselius. *March 22nd, 1871*

At sight of the room, perfectly undisturbed except for our violent entrance, we began to cool a little and soon recovered our senses sufficiently to dismiss the men. It had struck Mademoiselle that possibly Carmilla had been awakened by the uproar at her door, and in her first panic had jumped from her bed and hid herself in a press, or behind a curtain, from which she could not, of course, emerge until the major-domo and his myrmidons had withdrawn. We now recommenced our search and began to call her name again.

It was all to no purpose. Our perplexity and agitation increased. We examined the windows, but they were secured. I implored of Carmilla, if she had concealed herself, to play this cruel trick no longer—to come out and to end our anxieties. It was all useless. I was by this time convinced she was not in the room, nor in the dressing room, the door of which was still locked on this side. She could not have passed it. I was utterly puzzled. Had Carmilla discovered one of those secret passages which the old housekeeper said were known to exist in the schloss, although the knowledge of their exact location had been lost? A little time would no doubt explain all—utterly perplexed as for the present we were.

It was past four o'clock, and I preferred passing the remaining hours of darkness in Madame's room. Daylight brought no solution of the difficulty.

The whole household, with my father at its head, was in a state of agitation next morning. Every part of the chateau was searched. The grounds were explored. No trace of the missing lady could be discovered. The stream was about to be dragged; my father was in distraction; what a tale to have to tell the poor girl's mother on her return. I, too, was almost beside myself, though my grief of course was quite of a different kind.

The morning was passed in alarm and excitement. It was now one o'clock and still no tidings. I ran up to Carmilla's room and found her standing at her dressing table. I was astounded. I could not believe my eyes. She beckoned me to her with her pretty finger, in silence. Her face expressed extreme fear.

I ran to her in an ecstasy of joy; I kissed and embraced her again and again, tears of relief running down my cheeks. I ran to the bell and rang it vehemently, to bring others to the spot that might at once relieve my father's anxiety.

"Dear Carmilla, what has become of you all this time? We have been in agonies of anxiety about you," I exclaimed. "Where have you been? How did you come back?"

"Last night has been a night of wonders," she said.

"For mercy's sake, explain all you can," I implored.

"It was past two last night," she said, "when I went to sleep as usual in my bed, with my doors locked, that of the dressing room and that opening upon the gallery. My sleep was uninterrupted and as far as I know dreamless; but I woke just now on the sofa in the dressing room there, I found the door between the rooms open and the other door forced. How could all this have happened without my being wakened? It must have been accompanied with a great deal of noise, and I am particularly easily roused; and how could I have been carried out of my bed without my sleep having been interrupted, I whom the slightest stir startles?"

By this time, Madame, Mademoiselle, my father, and a number of the servants were in the room. Carmilla was, of course overwhelmed with inquiries, congratulations and welcomes. She had but one story to tell, and seemed the least able of all the party to suggest any way of accounting for what had happened.

My father took a turn up and down the room, thinking. I saw Carmilla's eyes follow him for a moment with a sly, dark glance.

When my father had sent the servants away, Mademoiselle having gone in search of a little bottle of valerian and Sal volatile, and there being no one now in the room with Carmilla, except my father, Madame and me, he came to her thoughtfully, took her hand very kindly, led her to the sofa and sat down beside her.

"Will you forgive me, my dear, if I risk a conjecture and ask a question?"

"Who can have a better right?" she said. "Ask what you please and I will tell you everything. But my story is simply one of bewilderment and darkness. I know absolutely nothing. Put any question you please, but you know of course, the limitations Mamma has placed me under."

"Perfectly, my dear child, I need not approach the topics on which she desires our silence. Now, the marvel of last night consists in your having been removed from your bed and your room, without being wakened, and this removal having occurred apparently while the windows were still secured and the two doors locked upon the inside. I will tell you my theory and ask you a question."

Carmilla was leaning on her hand dejectedly; Madame and I were listening breathlessly.

"Now, my question is this. Have you ever been suspected of walking in your sleep?"

"Never, since I was very young indeed."

"But you did walk in your sleep when you were young?"

"Yes; I know I did. I have been told so often by my old nurse."

My father smiled and nodded.

"Well then, my dear, what has happened is this. You got up in your sleep, unlocked the door, not leaving the key as usual in the lock, but taking it out and locking it on the outside; you again took the key out, carried it away with you to some one of the twenty five rooms on this floor, or perhaps upstairs or downstairs. There are so many rooms and closets, so much heavy furniture and such accumulations of lumber, that it would require a week to search this old house thoroughly. Do you see now what I mean?"

"I do, but not all," she answered.

"And how, Papa, do you account for her finding herself on the sofa in the dressing room, which we had searched so carefully?"

"She came there after you had searched it, still in her sleep, and at last awoke spontaneously, and was as much surprised to find herself where she was as any one else. I wish all mysteries were as easily and innocently explained as yours, Carmilla," he said, laughing. "And so we may congratulate ourselves on the certainty that the most natural explanation of the occurrence is one that involves no drugging, no tampering with locks, no burglars, or poisoners, or witches—nothing that need alarm Carmilla or anyone else, for our safety."

Carmilla was looking charmingly. Nothing could be more beautiful than her tints. Her beauty was, I think, enhanced by that graceful languor that was peculiar to her. I think my father was silently contrasting her looks with mine, for he said:

"I wish my poor Laura was looking more like herself," and he sighed.

So our alarms, at least on this occasion, were happily ended, and Carmilla restored to her friends.

Chapter 15

Excerpt from the journal of Doctor Alvinci, *August 26th, 1860*

It came as a measure of great relief to me when I first received word from Baron Vordenburg, which confirmed his willingness to 'help resolve this most pressing matter, and at the earliest possible opportunity.' Although I cannot stress enough, his assistance is now required as a matter of the gravest urgency, especially following the harrowing events of the preceding twenty four hours.

These occurrences, which I shall now set down for posterity, have left those who reside within this locale even more traumatised than had previously been the situation. All that we can do is pray that the Lord Almighty will instil Baron Vordenburg with the necessary fortitude to act as the vessel of our salvation, and with which to deliver us from the growing evil that consumes us.

In the early hours of this morning, Karl Bohm, the father of the dead peasant girl, Katharina, made a visit to the graveyard which sits next to the old chapel, and wherein resides the body of his beloved daughter. The cemetery's upkeep has been neglected for many years, its residents ignored since the chapel was abandoned almost sixty years ago. It is a fact that is easily noted by any who choose to walk there. These past weeks though, I fear the still hallowed grounds have seen too many young bodies interred therein. The peasants, it would seem, seek solace for their loss by placing their loved ones in the shadow of God's house.

Bohm, not unnaturally, had been having a great trouble sleeping since his confrontation with the fiend that was preying upon his poor child.

It was just shortly before dawn when Bohm arrived at his girl's graveside. He had stopped to pick some Edelweiss on his way to the churchyard, intent on making his daughter's tomb as pleasing to the eye, for any who should view it, as was possible.

The air was damp, and as he pushed open the old iron gate leading into the graveyard, he recalled that he became aware of a feeling of being observed.

He had not long been kneeling beside his child's grave, dead-heading the wilting flowers, arranging the Edelweiss amongst those blooms which still flourished, when the solitude of the morning was punctuated by the sound of bracken being broken heavily underfoot. This caused him to start, he looked to the direction of the noise; the graveyard is a most foreboding place, and never in his previous visits had he so much as heard a bird's song, or spotted a woodland creature running through the undergrowth. Always, it was a place of solitude.

The sight confronting the distraught father was enough to make him tumble from his knees, so that he ended in a sitting position; his back rested against the mound of his daughter's grave, his arms stretched crucifix style cradling the length of the elevated earth.

Just a few feet in front of him, a huge black wolf stared intently from behind baleful yellow eyes. It made no sound, other than the steady panting of its breath, which was accentuated by the rise and fall of its broad chest. Its jaw hung open, cruel lips drawn sneeringly back, revealing razor sharp canines which gleamed horribly in the early morning light. Droplets of sticky saliva dripped from the animal's long pink tongue, which lolled out one side of the beast's mouth.

Bohm had lived in this area his whole life, only three times previously had he ever seen a wolf, but never once anything so impossibly large as this animal. Terrified, he began to recite the Lord's Prayer, convinced of the fact that he was about to meet with his maker, and it was as he did so that he first laid eyes on the others. From out of the depths of the graveyard six more wolves appeared. They were all sturdy beasts. Steadily they moved closer to him, until the creatures joined ranks with the larger black wolf, encircling the grave upon which Bohm was prostrated.

At this moment Bohm believed his time to be up, but as frightened as the man was, he had never overcome the torment of losing his wife, and now he also mourned the loss of his most precious child.

He was a broken man, and so was readily prepared to accept whatever fate may have in store for him. Even if he was to suffer the horror of being torn apart and devoured, he would accept his lot, for he had failed in his duty as a parent, by failing to protect his beautiful Katharina. No, he deserved to die. At least, these were the thoughts that filled his brain, utterly mistaken as he was in thinking any of this madness was of his doing. However, these musings did not long weigh heavy on his mind.

Indeed, all thought of his own untimely demise was banished from his head the moment he glanced up and looked beyond the animals surrounding him. He saw an impossible vision of beauty. His jaw dropped in stunned disbelief, his eyes welling with tears of joy and surprise. Some fifty paces to his left, from between a row of mouldering gravestones, Katharina appeared; moving languidly among the tombstones, still dressed in her white funeral gown.

The girl looked pallid and weak, nonetheless it was definitely Katharina, and although seemingly lacking in vigour her movements contained a certain gracefulness. More importantly for Karl Bohm, she was alive. Or so it appeared.

Without thought, Bohm called out to Katharina, and instantly regretted his decision. One of the wolves, a sleek grey animal and quite possibly the smallest of the pack, turned away from the rest of the group and bounded at speed towards the girl, its body slung low to the ground as it moved into attack mode.

Bohm once again cried out to his daughter, this time intent on voicing a warning about the encroaching beast. He never completed his sentence. The words stuck in his throat, as what happened next defied all possible belief.

The wolf had closed the distance between itself and the girl, rapidly reaching a point just a few metres short of where she stood, before leaping into the air, intent on striking the throat of its intended prey. It failed miserably in its attack. Katharina, a slight girl of barely sixteen years, reached out her right arm and caught hold of the wolf, mid-leap. The wolf, although small in comparison to its compatriots, was nonetheless more than twice the size of the girl. Yet Bohm witnessed the surreal sight of his reanimated daughter, holding the wolf aloft by its throat. The girl reached out with her free hand and touched the creature, running her fingers through the soft fur atop its crown. She then gently fingered its ears, quizzically, as though studying the ever more frantically struggling animal.

Bohm's eyes fixated on the incapacitated wolf; it was only when he glanced once again at his daughter, he noticed the girl's features changing. Her visage was taking on a most horrid countenance. Katharina's father would later describe in his own words how his daughter's face had greater semblance to the features of a demon born of hell, than to anything resembling his child.

The wolf began to wretch, its hind legs kicking ever more frenetically as Katharina closed her fingers around its throat; squeezing the life from it. With her other hand she, with little or no effort, pulled off one of the creature's ears, and studied it intently, as a child might study one of spring's earliest blooms. She herself seemed surprised as to how easily the appendage had come away in her hand. The creature cried out in its distress. A most awful noise indeed according to Bohm, and as one the rest of the pack peeled away from the area around the graveside.

Bohm struggled to his feet, once again calling out a warning to the girl, although he was no longer truly convinced this thing was his daughter. He once again regretted his actions.

The girl responded to his cry, easily throwing the creature, which she had held in her hand, in the direction of the rapidly advancing pack. The injured wolf landed with a heavy thud, flooring two of its kin that had been unfortunate enough to break its fall. What now troubled Bohm more though, at the sound of his cry, the black wolf had stopped in its tracks and spun around to once again face him.

The thought entered his head that he should try to flee, but in truth he never had a chance. In an instant the creature was upon him. The pain that ran through his body was blinding, as the wolf bit into his torso. He felt his life fluids spurting freely from the left side of his torn body and kicked out at the creature in blind panic. Incredibly, he managed to dislodge the animal, albeit only briefly, and only then to feel even more intense pain as the wolf attacked again, this time sinking its jaws into his calf. Bohm screamed as the creature began shaking its head, attempting to tear off the leg that it held in its mouth, severing it from his broken body.

As the wolf shook him, Bohm was aware of an awful, rhythmic, cracking sound, and just before he lost consciousness he realised it was the sound of his own head repeatedly bouncing off the hard ground. One of his last recollections was of Katharina screaming in pain, and that the cry, although obviously that of his beautiful daughter, was tainted with a disturbing animalistic quality.

Karl Bohm had been a regular visitor to his sister's house since the death of his daughter. Astrid, and her husband Bernard, had been good to him. They had prepared his meals, and always insisted that he was never left alone long enough to drown in his thoughts. Astrid had become worried when her brother failed to show up for his breakfast, and knowing that he would have made pilgrimage to the graveyard, she quickly dispatched her spouse to search for him.

There was only a matter of hours between the time that Bernard found his wife's brother, and when he delivered the badly injured man into the care of Doctor Spielberg and I. Shaking though the poor man was, he told us of the horrors which had greeted him upon discovering his stricken brother in law.

Bohm was in a state of trauma; indeed it remains a mystery as to how he even managed to survive the attack of the wolf. We had to remove what remained of his damaged leg and infuse him with blood. Thankfully, Astrid is a woman of strong character, and she proved more than willing to act as our donor. Bohm is of an equally strong nature and will likely make a good recovery, at least in part. Indeed, by mid-afternoon he was able to supply us with his account of the events which I have just recited. By then of course, a party of local men, myself included, had already made a visit to the cemetery, Bernard's initial observations having piqued our collective interest.

The graveyard was a picture of carnage. Blood spattered tombstones smashed and broken and large clods of earth torn up and scattered around. It had obviously been the scene of a most robust struggle. A fact quickly confirmed by further exploration of the site, which soon revealed something both as mysterious as it was horrific.

One of the woodsmen who had accompanied us found, on the east side of the graveyard, the dismembered leg of a young female, likely of a similar age to Katharina. Further investigation revealed, scattered at geographic points around the graveyard, other limbs that had been torn from the body of a woman.

Bordering the circumference of the old chapel, we discovered shredded remnants of human torso, still partly clothed in white funeral linen. Gingerly, we entered the disused building, wherein we discovered a horror amongst horrors.

Impaled onto a brass cross, positioned just in front of the most forward pew, was the severed head of a young girl. Her features heavily bloodstained: even so I recognised immediately the face of Katharina Bohm, although to see such angst etched across that once pretty face shall surely haunt me till the very end of my days.

We had not yet at this time had Karl Bohm's version of events accounted to us, and so the mystery of what had occurred remained. There had obviously been a fierce struggle, and presumably the pack of wolves involved in this attack was the same animals that had done for the little mountebank. Was it possible these creatures were not acting randomly? Maybe they were being controlled by someone? How else could we explain the removal of their victims' heads, and the subsequent impalement of those heads? There were so many questions and yet so few answers.

The girl's grave was undisturbed, yet her body had been removed from it and subjected to a most pernicious assault; presumably, based on the positioning of the body parts, as part of some occult ritual. Yet still the strangest mystery persisted. The girl had been interred for a period of time, on the morning of her funeral I myself had paid my respects and she was cold with the touch of death. Yet now, even some hours after the dismembering of her body, the flesh was warm, and retained the pliability of touch consistent with that of a living being. I pride myself on being a believer that all manner of things are possible in this world. Was it really the case this poor child had in fact become a revenant, cursed to rise from the depths of her grave and seek prey amongst the living?

I fear Baron Vordenburg cannot arrive soon enough, for the horrors of this day were not yet done. One of the men who had accompanied us to the graveyard was Bruno Dorner, the swineherd whose young wife, Analiese, had also succumbed to the evil which is plaguing these lands. Upon hearing Karl Bohm's story late that afternoon, Bruno insisted on returning to the cemetery, intent on securing the sanctity of his wife's grave.

It was early evening by the time a dozen of us made our return to the graveyard, and each of us was armed in some way. I was lucky enough to be in possession of a smooth bore musket, which had once belonged to my father. A number of the peasants made use of more rustic armaments, such as wood axes and scythes. Although, in truth, none of us truly knew the nature of the foes we might face.

We were relieved to find Analiese's grave seemed to be undisturbed, Bruno though was not so easily satisfied. He made comment to the effect that the Bohm girl's grave had also appeared undisturbed, and yet her body had been desecrated around the graveyard.

It was under much duress, but nonetheless the decision was agreed at the grieving man's behest, to open up the grave of his dead wife, so that he might know she lay without violation, within the shadow of God's house.

Fortunately, old Fabian had been lacking of anything resembling a weapon within his cottage and so he had chosen to carry with him his sturdiest spade, convinced as he was that its sharp edge might offer him a modicum of protection, should the need arise. This being the only digging implement carried by our posse, it at least served to make our task more rapid, as did the fact we all took turns with digging out the grave.

When the hole was dug, and the coffin lifted clear, Bruno used his blade to lever out the pins holding shut the lid. As he opened the casket there was a collective gasp of shocked horror at the sight which greeted us. The box was empty.

Bruno was distraught, and understandably so. His wife had looked beautiful even in death, when laid to rest in her finest blue dress with its fine stitched trim. Truly, she had looked like a woman of higher standing, rather than the wife of a swineherd. Now though she was gone, and it presented us with yet another mystery.

There was no sign of the wolves having dug open her grave, indeed the box was still sealed and intact. Yet I myself witnessed the lid being nailed shut, and then after attended her burial. So the question now remains, what became of Analiese's body, and how was it removed from within a sealed grave? As I stated previously, so many questions remain and yet we have so few answers.

Chapter 16

Correspondence from Laura Bennett, addressed to Doctor Hesselius. *March 24th, 1871*

Following the incident when Carmilla was mislaid to us, my father took the decision to have an attendant sleep in her room; but Carmilla was totally opposed to this. Eventually Papa conceded, and as a compromise it was agreed a servant should sleep outside her door, so that she would not attempt to make another such excursion without being arrested at her own door.

The night passed quietly; and next morning early, the doctor, whom my father had sent for without telling me a word about it, arrived to see me.

Madame accompanied me to the library, and there to my surprise I found Doctor Spielberg, the grave little doctor, with white hair and spectacles, who had visited our home on many previous occasions, often just stopping by for a cup of tea and a bun, during the course of doing his rounds. I greeted him courteously, Madame then informing me that the doctor had actually called to visit with me.

I told him my story, and as I proceeded he grew graver and graver.

We were standing, he and I, in the recess of one of the windows, facing one another. When my statement was over, he leaned with his shoulders against the wall, and with his eyes fixed on me earnestly, with an interest in which was a dash of horror.

After a minute's reflection, he asked Madame if he could see my father.

He was sent for accordingly, and as he entered, smiling, he said: "I dare say, doctor, you are going to tell me that I am an old fool for having brought you here. I hope I am."

But his smile faded into shadow as the doctor, with a very grave face, beckoned him closer.

He and the doctor talked for some time in the same recess where I had just conferred with the physician. It seemed an earnest and argumentative conversation. The room is very large, and Madame and I stood together, burning with curiosity at the farther end. Our ears strained, though barely a word were we able to hear clearly, although Madame insisted she heard the name of Doctor Alvinci, the tall man who had visited us previously, mentioned on a couple of occasions. They spoke in a very low tone, the deep recess of the window quite concealed the doctor from view, very nearly my father too, whose foot, arm and shoulder only could we see; and the voices were, I suppose, all the less audible for the sort of closet which the thick wall and window formed.

After a time my father's face looked into the room; it was pale, thoughtful, and I fancied agitated.

"Laura dear, come here for a moment. Madame, we shan't trouble you the doctor says, at present."

Accordingly I approached, for the first time a little alarmed, for although I felt very weak, I did not feel ill; and strength, one always fancies, is a thing that may be picked up when we please.

My father held out his hand to me as I drew near, but he was looking at the doctor, and he said:

"It certainly is very odd; I don't understand it quite. Laura, come here, dear; now pay attention to Doctor Spielberg, and recollect yourself."

"You mentioned a sensation like that of two needles piercing your skin somewhere about your neck, on the night when you experienced your first horrible dream. Is there still any soreness?"

"None at all," I answered.

"Can you indicate with your finger about the point at which you think this occurred?"

"Very little below my throat—here," I answered.

I wore a morning dress, which covered the place I pointed to.

"Now you can satisfy yourself," said the doctor. "You won't mind your papa lowering your dress a very little. It is necessary, to detect a symptom of the complaint under which you may have been suffering."

I acquiesced. It was only an inch or two below the edge of my collar.

"God bless me—so it is," exclaimed my father, growing pale.

The doctor nodded his affirmation. "You see it now with your own eyes," he said, with a gloomy triumph.

"What is it?" I exclaimed, beginning to be frightened.

"Nothing, my dear young lady, but a small blue spot about the size of the tip of your little finger; and now," he continued, turning to Papa, "the question is what is best to be done?"

"Is there any danger?" I urged, in great trepidation.

"I trust not, my dear," answered the doctor. "I don't see why you should not recover. I don't see why you should not begin immediately to get better."

His words lacked conviction.

"That is the point at which the sense of strangulation begins?" he continued.

"Yes," I answered.

"And—recollect as well as you can—the same point was a kind of centre of that thrill which you described just now, like the current of a cold stream running against you?"

"It may have been; I think it was."

"Ay, you see?" he added, turning to my father. "Shall I say a word to Madame?"

"Certainly," said my father.

He called Madame to him, and said:

"I find my young friend here far from well. It won't be of any great consequence I hope; but it will be necessary that some steps be taken, which I will explain by-and-by; but in the meantime,

Madame, you will be so good as not to let Miss Laura be alone for one moment. That is the only direction I need give for the present. It is indispensable."

"We may rely upon your kindness, Madame, I know," added my father.

Madame satisfied him eagerly.

"And you, dear Laura, I know you will observe the doctor's direction."

"Yes, of course," I replied, nodding acceptance of my father's instruction.

"I shall have to ask your opinion upon another patient, whose symptoms slightly resemble those of my daughter, that have just been detailed to you—very much milder in degree, but I believe quite of the same sort. She is a young lady—our guest; but as you say you will be passing this way again this evening, you can't do better than take your supper here and you can then see her. She does not come down till the afternoon."

"I thank you," said the doctor. "I shall be with you then, at about seven this evening."

And then they repeated their directions to me and to Madame, and with this parting charge my father left us, walked out with the doctor; and I saw them pacing together up and down between the road and the moat, on the grassy platform in front of the castle, evidently absorbed in earnest conversation.

The doctor did not return. I saw him mount his horse there, take his leave, and ride away eastward through the forest.

Nearly at the same time I saw the man arrive from Dranfield with the letters, and dismount and hand the bag to my father.

In the meantime, Madame and I were both busy, lost in conjecture as to the reasons of the singular and earnest direction which the doctor and my father had concurred in imposing. Madame, as she afterwards told me, was afraid the doctor feared the onset of a sudden seizure, and that without prompt assistance; I might either lose my life in a fit, or at least be seriously hurt.

The interpretation did not strike me; and I fancied, perhaps luckily for my nerves, that the arrangement was prescribed simply to secure a companion, who would prevent my taking too much exercise, eating unripe fruit, or doing any of the fifty foolish things to which young people are supposed to be prone.

About half an hour after my father came in—he had a letter in his hand—and said:

"This letter had been delayed; it is from General Spielsdorf. He might have been here yesterday, he may not come till tomorrow or he may be here today."

He put the open letter into my hand; but he did not look pleased, as he usually did when a guest, especially one so much loved as the General was coming. On the contrary, he looked as if he wished him at the bottom of the Red Sea. There was plainly something on his mind which he did not choose to divulge.

"Papa, darling, will you tell me this?" said I, suddenly laying my hand on his arm, and looking, I am sure, imploringly in his face.

"Perhaps?" he answered, smoothing my hair caressingly over my eyes.

"Does the doctor think me very ill?"

"No, dear; he thinks, if right steps are taken you will be quite well again. At least on the high road to a complete recovery in a day or two, and he further intends to confer details of your condition with his colleague, Doctor Alvinci, who is a very more learned man on matters such as these," he answered, a little dryly. "I wish our good friend the General had chosen any other time; that is, I wish you had been perfectly well to receive him," he added, almost as an afterthought.

"But do tell me, Papa," I insisted, "what does he think is the matter with me?"

"Nothing; you must not plague me with questions," he answered, with more irritation than I ever remember him displaying before; and seeing that I looked wounded, I suppose, he kissed me and added, "You shall know all about it in a day or two; this is all that I know. In the meantime you are not to trouble your head about it."

He turned and left the room, but came back before I had done wondering and puzzling over the oddity of all this. It was merely to say that he was going to Karnstein, and had ordered the carriage to be ready at twelve, and that I and Madame should accompany him. He intended on going to see the priest who lived near those picturesque grounds, as there was business to discuss. As Carmilla had never seen them, she could follow when she came down, with Mademoiselle, who would bring materials for what you call a picnic, which might be laid for us in the ruined castle.

At twelve o'clock, accordingly, I was ready and not long after, my father, Madame and I set out upon our projected drive. It surprised me greatly to find that as well as the coachman, our party was also to be accompanied by two of the stoutest male servants, one of whom; being an ex military man, was proficient in the use of a smooth bore musket; which he carried on a shoulder strap. The other fellow wielded a formidable looking axe. It was only later, when I learned of the wolf pack which had been so terrorising our neighbourhood, that I understood Papa's decision to have armed men escort us during our journey to Karnstein. Passing the drawbridge we turned to the right, followed the road over the steep Gothic bridge westward, to reach the deserted village and ruined castle of Karnstein.

No sylvan drive can be fancied prettier. The ground breaks into gentle hills and hollows all clothed with beautiful wood, totally destitute of the comparative formality which artificial planting, early culture, and pruning impart.

The irregularities of the ground often lead the road out of its course, and cause it to wind beautifully round the sides of broken hollows and the steeper sides of the hills, among varieties of ground almost inexhaustible.

Turning one of these points, we suddenly encountered our old friend the General, riding towards us. He was attended by a mounted servant, who himself looked to be in need of some care, a sizeable bandage swathing one side of his head and face. The General's portmanteaus followed in a hired wagon, such as we term a cart, which also contained what I could only describe as half a dozen of the most brutish looking men I had ever seen. Each one looked to have murder in their eyes, and there demeanour suggested to me they might be mercenaries. Although in truth, I had only ever read of such roguish men of war.

The General dismounted as we pulled up, and, after the usual greetings, was easily persuaded to accept the vacant seat in our carriage. He suggested that his mounted companion, who was a boy of no more advanced years than I, should escort our carriage, and then instructed that his own horse should be sent on with his other servants to the schloss.

Chapter 17

Correspondence from Laura Bennett, addressed to Doctor Hesselius. *March 24th, 1871*

It was about ten months since we had last seen the General, but that time had sufficed to make an alteration of years in his appearance. He had grown thinner; something of gloom and anxiety having taken the place of that cordial serenity which used to characterize his features. His dark blue eyes, always penetrating, now gleamed with a sterner light from under his furrowed brow. It was not such a change as grief alone usually induces, and angrier passions seemed to have had their share in bringing it about.

We had not long resumed our drive when the General began to talk with his usual soldierly directness of the bereavement, as he termed it, sustained in the death of his one true beloved. He then broke out in a tone of intense bitterness and fury; inveighing against the "hellish arts" to which she had fallen victim, and expressing with more exasperation than piety how his betrothed had brought him understanding that all forms of life have the right to be considered sacred. It was an observation which he confessed, as a military man he had never truly given much consideration to. Still though, he wondered how it was that heaven should tolerate so monstrous an indulgence of the lusts and malignity of hell.

My father, who saw at once that something very extraordinary had befallen, asked, if not too painful for him, to detail the circumstances which he thought justified the strong terms in which he expressed himself.

"Thomas, my old friend, I should tell you all with pleasure," said the General, "but you would not believe me!"

"Why should I not?" he asked.

"Because," he answered testily, "you believe in nothing but things consistent with your own prejudices and illusions. I remember when I was like you, but I have since learned better."

"Try me," said my father, "I am not such a dogmatist as you suppose. Besides which, I very well know that you generally require proof for what you believe, and am therefore very strongly predisposed to respect your conclusions."

"You are right in supposing that I have not been led lightly into a belief in the marvellous—for what I have experienced is marvellous indeed—and horrific too! I have been forced by extraordinary evidence to credit that which ran counter, diametrically, to all my theories. I have been made the dupe of a preternatural conspiracy."

Notwithstanding his professions of confidence in the General's penetration, I saw my father, at this point, glance at the General with, as I thought, a marked suspicion of his sanity.

The General did not see it, luckily. He was looking gloomily and curiously into the glades and vistas of the woods that were opening before us.

"You are going to the ruins of Karnstein?" he said. "Yes, it is a lucky coincidence; do you know I was going to ask you to bring me there to inspect them. I have been in correspondence with an old acquaintance about this place. Indeed, he assures me that he too intends on making this selfsame journey, and we both have a special objective in exploring. There is a ruined chapel, isn't there, with a great many tombs of that extinct family?"

"So there are—highly interesting," said my father. "I hope you are thinking of claiming the title and estates?"

My father said this gaily, but the General did not recollect the laugh, or even the smile, which courtesy exacts for a friend's joke. On the contrary, he looked grave and even fierce, ruminating on a matter that stirred his anger and horror.

"Something very different," he said, gruffly. "I mean to unearth some of those fine people. I hope, by God's blessing, to accomplish a pious sacrilege here, which will relieve our earth of certain monsters, and enable honest people to sleep in their beds without being assailed by murderers. I have strange things to tell you, my dear friend, such as I myself would have discounted as incredible barely more than twelve months ago."

My father looked at him again, but this time not with a glance of suspicion—with an eye, rather, of keen intelligence and alarm.

"The house of Karnstein," replied my father, "has been long extinct: a hundred years at least. My dear wife was maternally descended from the Karnsteins. But the name and title have long ceased to exist. The castle is a ruin; the very village is deserted; it is many long years since the smoke of a chimney was seen there; not a roof left."

"Quite true, I have heard a great deal about that since I last saw you; a great deal that will astonish you. But I had better relate everything in the order in which it occurred," said the General. "I know it was but once that you saw my darling Bertha, but surely you would agree, no creature could ever have been more beautiful, and only three months ago none more blooming."

"Yes, poor thing! When I saw her last she certainly was quite lovely," said my father. "I was grieved and shocked more than I can tell you, my dear friend; I knew what a blow it was to you."

He took the General's hand, and they exchanged a kind pressure. Tears gathered in the old soldier's eyes. He did not seek to conceal them.

He said: "Thomas, ours is a very old friendship; I knew you would feel for me, as I was edging towards a lifetime of forlorn years. But she had become an object of very dear interest to me, and repaid my care by an affection that cheered my soul and made my life happy. That is all gone. The years that remain to me on earth will not, I hope, be very long. I have no wish for a life without my beloved; but by God's mercy I hope to accomplish a service to mankind before I end my days, and to sub-serve the vengeance of heaven upon the fiends who have murdered my poor darling who was still in the spring of her hopes and beauty!"

"You said, just now, that you intended relating everything as it occurred," said my father. "Pray do; I assure you that it is not mere curiosity that prompts me."

By this time we had reached the point at which the Drunstall road, by which the General had come, diverges from the road which we were travelling to Karnstein.

"How far is it to the ruins?" enquired the General, looking anxiously forward.

"About half a league," answered my father. "Pray let us hear the story you were so good as to promise."

Chapter 18

Excerpt from the journal of Doctor Alvinci, *September 4th, 1860*

Last night a rider arrived, carrying with him fresh dispatches from the good Baron Vordenburg, and at last it would seem that we are closing in on the source of the evil which plagues these lands.

The Baron had asked me to meet with him at the home of Father Wagner, a priest who lives two miles east of the Karnstein ruins. The intention is for us to travel on to Karnstein, and he informed me that we will be met there by one other. The man we will be meeting is General Spielsdorf, and unbeknownst to the Baron, the General and I are already acquainted, having met recently during the time of his great tragedy. It intrigues me as to the circumstances which bring the General in the direction of Karnstein. It also pains me still that I was unable to do more, in order that his beautiful lady might have survived the horror which afflicted her.

I cannot now help but wonder; mayhap this evil we face is indeed tied in with the very fiend the good General has been in pursuit of? Although I understood that his searches had taken him off in a different direction. Whatever the case, perchance we two have far better success on this occasion.

I did not settle well last night in anticipation of whatever horrors this day may bring, and so it was at dawn's first light that I set off for Father Wagner's home. Baron Vordenburg arrived barely an hour later than I, accompanied by a formidable looking entourage of a dozen men, all of whom, although casually dressed, bore arms and conducted themselves with the demeanour of military men.

After we had taken a brief time to re-establish our acquaintances and partake of refreshments, we three proceeded to spend the morning talking in earnest, devising a necessary plan of action.

The Baron had requested some antiquated maps of the ruins be delivered to this abode; unfortunately, the dispatches have as yet failed to arrive. We have taken the decision to hold back, until after lunch, in the hope the rider makes due haste. The Baron is adamant that we require these maps, so as best to achieve our goal. However, he is in agreement that should they fail to arrive, we will proceed on to Karnstein without them, in the hope that fate may grant us the boon of chancing upon that which we seek.

Chapter 19

Correspondence from Laura Bennett, addressed to Doctor Hesselius. *March 24th, 1871*

It was with a huge sigh, which betrayed his aching heart; the General began to relate his story.

"With all my heart," said the General, with much effort, and after pausing just long enough to steady himself and arrange his subject, he commenced one of the strangest narratives I ever heard.

"My dear Bertha had not been long recovered from the effects of a seasonal malady, which had laid her low, raising her temperature and dulling her senses for a good few days. Now though, she was well on the path to recovery and looking forward, with great pleasure, to the visit you had been so good as to arrange for her to your charming daughter."

Here he made me a gallant but melancholy bow.

"In the meantime we had an invitation to my old friend the Count Carlsfield, whose schloss is about six leagues to the other side of Karnstein. It was to attend the series of fetes which, you will remember, were given by him in honour of his most illustrious visitor, the Grand Duke Charles."

"Yes, and very splendid I believe they were," said my father.

"Princely! But then his hospitalities are quite regal. He has Aladdin's lamp. The night from which my sorrow dates was devoted to a magnificent masquerade. The grounds were thrown open, the trees hung with coloured lamps. There was such a display of fireworks as Paris itself had never witnessed. And such music—music, you know is my weakness—such ravishing music the band did play! The finest instrumental band, perhaps, in the world, and the finest singers who could be collected from all the great operas in Europe. As you wandered through these fantastically illuminated grounds, the moon-lighted chateau throwing a rosy light from its long rows of windows, you would suddenly hear these ravishing voices stealing from the silence of some grove, or rising from boats upon the lake. I felt myself, as I looked and listened, carried back into the romance and poetry of my early youth."

"It was a grand night indeed then, my old friend."

"Yes, yes indeed, and when the fireworks were ended, and the ball beginning, we returned to the noble suite of rooms that were thrown open to the dancers. A masked ball, you know, is a beautiful sight; but so brilliant a spectacle of the kind I never saw before," the General paused, as though swept away amongst his own thoughts.

My father waited patiently, unwilling to hasten his old friend's recollections.

Finally the General spoke. "It was a very aristocratic assembly. I was myself almost the only 'nobody' present." His features had warmed into a half smile, but his countenance swiftly returned to gloom as he continued. "My dear Bertha was looking quite beautiful. She wore no mask. Her excitement and delight added an unspeakable charm to her features; always lovely. I observed a young lady, dressed magnificently but wearing a mask, who appeared to me to be observing my beloved with extraordinary interest. I had seen her earlier in the evening in the great hall, and again for a few minutes walking near us, on the terrace under the castle windows, similarly employed. A lady, also masked; richly and gravely dressed, with a stately air like a person of rank, accompanied her as a chaperon. Had the young lady not worn a mask, I could of course have been much more certain upon the question; whether she was really watching my poor darling. I am now well assured that she was."

My father leaned forward in his seat, a look of concern clearly etched upon his face.

"We were now in one of the salons. My poor love had been dancing, and was now resting a little in one of the chairs near the door; I was standing near. The two ladies I have mentioned had approached and the younger took the chair next to Bertha; while her companion stood beside me, and for a little time addressed herself, in a low tone, to her charge."

"You spoke with this person?" asked my father.

"Indeed. After availing herself of the privilege of her mask, she turned to me, and in the tone of an old friend calling me by my name, opened a conversation with me, which piqued my curiosity a good deal. She referred to many scenes where she had met me—at Court, and at distinguished houses. She alluded to little incidents which I had long ceased to think of, but which I found had only lain in abeyance in my memory, for they instantly started into life at her touch."

"But she declined to introduce herself?"

The General nodded, "That's right old friend. I became more and more curious to ascertain who she was, every moment. She parried my attempts to discover very adroitly and pleasantly. The knowledge she showed of many passages in my life seemed to me all but unaccountable; and she appeared to take a not unnatural pleasure in foiling my curiosity and in seeing me flounder in my eager perplexity, from one conjecture to another."

I looked once more at my father, and the worry on his face concerned me greatly. I took hold of and gently squeezed his hand; he reciprocated and flashed me a comforting smile, although this did not placate me as I could tell that his actions were constrained. I glanced out the window, hoping to gain solace from the vista. Instead my eyes locked with those of the General's young companion, who rode alongside our carriage, and I was struck by the look of hatred that the youth's features displayed towards me. I quickly averted my gaze.

"In the meantime," continued the General, "the young lady, whom her mother called by the odd name of Millarca; when she once or twice addressed her, had with the same ease and grace, got into conversation with my beloved. She introduced herself by saying that her mother was a very old acquaintance of mine. She spoke of the agreeable audacity which a mask rendered practicable; she talked like a friend; she admired her dress and insinuated very prettily her admiration of her beauty. She pleasured her with laughing criticisms upon the people who crowded the ballroom, and laughed gaily at Bertha's amusement. She was very witty and lively when she pleased, after a time they had grown very good friends, and the young stranger lowered her mask, displaying a remarkably beautiful face. I had never seen it before, neither had my beloved. But though it was new to us, the features were so engaging, as well as lovely, that it was impossible not to feel the attraction powerfully. My poor girl did so. I never saw anyone more taken with another at first sight, unless indeed, it was the stranger herself, who seemed quite to have lost her heart to Bertha's affection."

The carriage hit a bump in the road, which momentarily came close to dislodging us from where we sat. After taking a moment to recompose ourselves, the General proceeded with his story.

"And so," he continued, "availing myself the license of a masquerade, I put not a few questions to the elder lady.

"'You have puzzled me utterly,' I said to her, laughing. 'Is that not enough? Won't you now consent to stand on equal terms, and grant me the kindness of removing your mask?'

"'Can any request be more unreasonable?' she replied. 'Ask a lady to yield an advantage! Besides, how do you know you should recognize me? Years make changes.'

"She seemed very reluctant to divulge herself," offered my father, knowingly.

"Indeed. But I was at that time still prepared to indulge her little game. 'As you see,' I said to her with a bow, and I suppose a rather melancholy little laugh, 'the years do indeed force changes upon us all.'

"'As philosophers tell us,' she said; 'and how do you know that a sight of my face would help you?'

"'I should take chance for that,' I answered. 'It is vain trying to make yourself out an old woman; your figure betrays you.'

"'Years, nevertheless, have passed since I saw you, rather since you saw me, for that is what I am considering. Millarca, there, is my daughter; I cannot then be young, even in the opinion of people whom time has taught to be indulgent, and I may not like to be compared with what you remember me. You have no mask to remove. You can offer me nothing in exchange.'

"'My petition is to your pity, to remove it.'

"'And mine to yours, to let it stay where it is,' she replied.

"'Well then, at least you will tell me whether you are French or German; you speak both languages so perfectly.'

"'I don't think I shall tell you that, General; you intend a surprise and are meditating the particular point of attack.'

"'At all events, you won't deny this,' I said, 'that being honoured by your permission to converse; I ought to know how to address you. Shall I say Madame la Comtesse?'

"She laughed, and she would no doubt have met me with another evasion—if, indeed, I can treat any occurrence in an interview every circumstance of which was prearranged, as I now believe, with the profoundest cunning, as liable to be modified by accident.

"'As to that,' she began; but she was interrupted, almost as she opened her lips, by a gentleman dressed in black, who looked particularly elegant and distinguished, with the drawback that his face was the most deadly pale I ever saw; except in death. He was in no masquerade—in the plain evening dress of a gentleman; and he said, without a smile, but with a courtly and unusually low bow:—

"'Will Madame la Comtesse permit me to say a very few words which may interest her?'

"The lady turned quickly to him, and touched her lip in token of silence; she then said to me, 'Keep my place for me, General; I shall return when I have said a few words.'

"And with this injunction, playfully given, she walked a little aside with the gentleman in black and talked for some minutes, apparently very earnestly. They then walked away slowly together in the crowd, and I lost them for some minutes.

"I spent the interval in cudgelling my brains for a conjecture as to the identity of the lady who seemed to remember me so kindly, and I was thinking of turning about and joining in the conversation between my beloved and the Countess's daughter, and trying whether, by the time she returned, I might not have a surprise in store for her; by having her name, title, chateau, and estates at my fingers' ends. But at this moment she returned, accompanied by the pale man in black, who said:

"'I shall return and inform Madame la Comtesse when her carriage is at the door.' He withdrew with a bow."

Chapter 20

Correspondence from Laura Bennett, addressed to Doctor Hesselius. *March 24th, 1871*

As the good General continued with reciting his tale of woe, I could not help but dwell upon the look of sorrow on his face. He had always been a sturdy fellow, imbued with the inner strength that can be so indicative of a man who has seen military service. Now though, he seemed devoid of all those old qualities. His face looked drawn, he sat, shoulders stooped, and hands clasped together, looking every inch a broken man.

"Please, good friend, continue with your story," urged my father, as the General once again fell silent, drifting off on his memories.

The General scratched his chin, fingernails rasping against day old stubble, "Very well then." he muttered. "After the pale man in black had departed from the lady and me, I turned to her and with a low bow asked the question, 'Are we then to lose Madame la Comtesse? If needs must then I can but hope it will be only for a few hours.'

"'It may be that only, or it may be a few weeks. It was very unlucky his speaking to me just now as he did. Do you now know me?'

"I assured her I did not.

"'You shall know me,' she said, 'but not at present. We are older and better friends than perhaps you suspect. I cannot yet declare myself. I shall in three weeks pass your beautiful schloss, about which I have been making enquiries. I shall then look in upon you for an hour or two, and renew a friendship which I never think of without a thousand pleasant recollections. But for this moment a piece of news has reached me like a thunderbolt. I must set out now, and travel by a devious route nearly a hundred miles, with all the dispatch I can possibly make. My perplexities multiply. I am only deterred by the compulsory reserve I practice as to my name from making a very singular request of you. My poor child has not quite recovered her strength. Her horse fell with her, at a hunt which she had ridden out to witness. Her nerves have not yet recovered the shock, and our physician says that she must on no account exert herself for some time to come. We came here, in consequence, by very easy stages—hardly six leagues a day. I must now travel day and night, on a mission of life and death—a mission the critical and momentous nature of which I shall be able to explain to you when next we meet, as I hope we shall in a few weeks, without the necessity of any concealment.'

"She went on to make her petition, and it was in the tone of a person from whom such a request amounted to conferring, rather than seeking a favour. This was only in manner, and, as it seemed, quite unconsciously. Then the terms in which it was expressed, nothing could be more deprecatory. It was simply that I would consent to take charge of her daughter during her absence.

"This was, all things considered, a strange, not to say an audacious request. She in some sort disarmed me, by stating and admitting everything that could be urged against it, and throwing herself entirely upon my chivalry. At the same moment, by a fatality that seems to have predetermined all that happened, my poor betrothed came to my side, and in an undertone, besought me to invite her new friend, Millarca, to pay us a visit. She had just been sounding her, and thought if her mamma would allow her, she would like it extremely.

"At another time I should have told her to wait a little, until at least we knew who they were. But I had not a moment to think in. The two ladies assailed me together, and I must confess the refined and beautiful face of the young lady; about which there was something extremely engaging, as well as the elegance and fire of high birth, determined me. Quite overpowered; I submitted and undertook too easily the care of the young lady, whom her mother called Millarca.

"The Countess beckoned to her daughter, who listened with grave attention while she told her, in general terms, how suddenly and peremptorily she had been summoned, and also of the arrangement she had made for her under my care, adding that I was one of her earliest and most valued friends.

"I made, of course, such speeches as the case seemed to call for, and found myself, on reflection, in a position which I did not half like.

"The gentleman in black returned, and very ceremoniously conducted the lady from the room.

"The demeanour of this gentleman was such as to impress me with the conviction that the Countess was a lady of very much more importance than her modest title alone might have led me to assume.

"Her last charge to me was that no attempt was to be made to learn more about her than I might have already guessed, until her return. Our distinguished host, whose guest she was, knew her reasons.

"'But here,' she said, 'neither I nor my daughter could safely remain for more than a day. I removed my mask imprudently for a moment, about an hour ago, and too late; I fancied you saw me. So I resolved to seek an opportunity of talking a little to you. Had I found that you had seen me, I would have thrown myself on your high sense of honour to keep my secret some weeks. As it is, I am satisfied that you did not see me; but if you now suspect, or on reflection, should suspect who I am, I commit myself in like manner, entirely to your honour. My daughter will observe the same secrecy, and I well know that you will from time to time remind her, lest she should thoughtlessly disclose it.'

"She whispered a few words to her daughter, kissed her hurriedly twice, and went away, accompanied by the pale gentleman in black, disappearing into the crowd.

"'In the next room,' said Millarca, 'there is a window that looks upon the hall door. I should like to see the last of mamma and to kiss my hand to her.'

"We assented of course and accompanied her to the window. We looked out and saw a handsome old-fashioned carriage; with a troop of couriers and footmen. We saw the slim figure of the pale gentleman in black, as he held a thick velvet cloak and placed it about her shoulders and threw the hood over her head. She nodded to him, and just touched his hand with hers. He bowed low repeatedly as the door closed, and the carriage began to move.

"'She is gone,' said Millarca, with a sigh.

"'She is gone,' I repeated to myself, for the first time—in the hurried moments that had elapsed since my consent—reflecting upon the folly of my act.

"'She did not look up,' said the young lady, plaintively.

"'The Countess had taken off her mask, perhaps, and did not care to show her face,' I said; 'and she could not know that you were in the window.'

"She sighed, and looked in my face. She was so beautiful that I relented. I was sorry I had for a moment repented of my hospitality, and I determined to make her amends for the un-avowed churlishness of my reception.

"The young lady, replacing her mask, joined Bertha in persuading me to return to the grounds; where the concert was soon to be renewed. We did so, and walked up and down the terrace that lies under the castle windows. Millarca became very intimate with us, and amused us with lively descriptions and stories of most of the great people whom we saw upon the terrace. I liked her more and more every minute. Her gossip without being ill-natured was extremely diverting to me, who had been so long out of the great world. I thought what essence she would give to Bertha, who for much of her life had been spared the company of other young women, and was now confined to sharing her evenings at home with an old soldier. Bertha's experience of being around women of her age could at best be described as limited; it would do her a world of good to mix in the company of Millarca. At least, this was what I foolishly believed at the time. And it was a belief that was further strengthened by Bertha's insistence that in Millarca she had truly found a kindred spirit. Oh my poor darling, how very wrong we both were.

"The ball was not over until the morning sun had almost cleared the horizon. It pleased the Grand Duke to dance till then, so loyal people could not go away, or think of bed. We had just got through a crowded saloon, when Bertha asked me what had become of Millarca. I thought she had been by her side, and she fancied she was by mine. The fact was we had lost her.

"All my efforts to find her were vain. I feared that she had mistaken, in the confusion of a momentary separation from us, other people for her new friends, and had possibly pursued and lost them in the extensive grounds which were thrown open to us.

"Now, in its full force, I recognized a new folly in my having undertaken the charge of a young lady without so much as knowing her name; and fettered as I was by promises, with reasons for imposing of which I knew nothing. I could not even point my inquiries by saying that the missing young lady was the daughter of the Countess, who had taken her departure a few hours before.

"Morning broke. It was clear daylight before I gave up my search. It was not till near two o'clock next day that we heard anything of my missing charge.

"At about that time a servant knocked at the door of our rooms, to say that he had been earnestly requested by a young lady, who appeared to be in great distress, to make out where she could find the General Baron Spielsdorf, and the young woman who was his betrothed, in whose charge she had been left by her mother.

"There could be no doubt, notwithstanding the slight inaccuracy, that indeed our young friend had turned up; and so she had. Would to heaven we had lost her!

"She told my poor Bertha a story to account for her having failed to recover us for so long. Very late, she said, she had got to the housekeeper's bedroom in despair of finding us, and had then fallen into a deep sleep which, long as it was, had hardly sufficed to recruit her strength after the fatigues of the ball.

"That day, Millarca came home with us. I was only too happy, after all, to have secured so charming a companion for my dear future wife."

Chapter 21

Correspondence from Laura Bennett, addressed to Doctor Hesselius. *March 24th, 1871*

As we closed in on our destination, the Karnstein ruins, I continued to listen intently to the ever more angst ridden recital of our friend the General, whilst every now and again sneaking a sideways glance in the direction of the young outrider. I was relieved to find that he no longer saw fit to fix me with his icy stare, although he still had a look of unpleasantness etched upon his face.

"So," asked my father, directing his question toward the General, "tell me how things changed for you once Millarca arrived?"

"Her arrival swiftly brought with it some drawbacks. In the first place, she complained of extreme languor—the weakness that remained after her late illness—and she never emerged from her room till the afternoon was pretty far advanced. In the next place, it was accidentally discovered, although she always locked her door on the inside and never disturbed the key from its place till she admitted the maid to assist at her toilet, that she was undoubtedly sometimes absent from her room in the very early morning, and at various times later in the day, before she wished it to be understood that she was stirring. She was repeatedly seen from the windows of the schloss, in the first faint grey of the morning, walking through the trees; in an easterly direction, and looking like a person in a trance. This convinced me that she walked in her sleep. But this hypothesis did not solve the puzzle. How did she pass out from her room, leaving the door locked on the inside? How did she escape from the house without unbarring door or window..?"

"Please my friend, proceed," urged my father, shifting forward in his seat.

"In the midst of my perplexities, an anxiety of a far more urgent kind started to present itself. My darling Bertha began to lose her looks and health, and that in a manner so mysterious, and even horrible, that I became thoroughly frightened.

"She was at first visited by appalling dreams; then, as she fancied, by a spectre, sometimes resembling Millarca, sometimes in the shape of a beast, indistinctly seen, walking round the foot of her bed, from side to side. Lastly there came sensations. One, not unpleasant, but very peculiar, she said, resembled the flow of an icy stream against her breast. At a later time she felt something like a pair of large needles piercing her, a little below the throat, inflicting a very sharp pain. A few nights after followed a gradual and convulsive sense of strangulation; then came unconsciousness."

I could hear distinctly every word the kind General was saying, without having to strain my ears, because by this time we were driving upon the short grass which spreads on either side of the road as you approach the roofless village, which had not shown the smoke of a chimney for more than a century.

You may guess how strangely I felt, as I heard my own symptoms so exactly described in those which had been experienced by the poor young woman who, but for the catastrophe which followed, would have been at that moment a visitor at my father's chateau. You may suppose also, how I felt as I heard him detail habits and mysterious peculiarities which were in fact those of our beautiful guest, Carmilla!

A vista opened in the forest; we were all of a sudden under the chimneys and gables of the ruined village, and the towers and battlements of the dismantled castle, around which gigantic trees are grouped, overhanging us from a slight eminence.

In a frightened reverie I got down from the carriage. Father instructed one of the servants to chaperon our group, whilst the driver and the servant who wielded the axe were ordered to stay behind and safeguard the horses. The General ordered his companion to remain also, although the stark look in the man's eyes suggested to me that he was far from pleased to receive such instructions. I fancied that maybe the General had noted the disdain with which his companion was once again viewing me. Then the four of us, trailed by the armed servant, set off in silence, for we each had abundant matter of thinking to do; we soon mounted the ascent, and were among the spacious chambers, winding stairs, and dark corridors of the castle.

"And this was once the palatial residence of the Karnsteins!" said the General at length, as from a great window he looked out across the village and saw the wide undulating expanse of forest.

"It was a bad family, and here its bloodstained annals were written," he continued. "It is hard that they should after death; continue to plague the human race with their atrocious lusts. That I believe is the chapel of the Karnsteins, down there."

He pointed down to the grey walls of the Gothic building partly visible through the foliage, a little way down the steep. "And I hear the axe of a woodman," he added, "busy among the trees that surround it; he possibly may give us the information of which I am in search, and point out the grave of Mircalla, Countess of Karnstein. These rustics preserve the local traditions of great families, whose stories die out among the rich and titled so soon as the families they become extinct."

"We have a portrait at home of Mircalla, the Countess Karnstein; should you like to see it?" asked my father.

"Time enough, dear friend," replied the General. "I believe that I have seen the original; and one motive which has led me to you earlier than I at first intended, was to explore the chapel which we are now approaching. My hand has been forced these past weeks. I have done things, and made bargains of which I am not proud. There is though, an evil that spreads through these lands, and sometimes, in order to clean up a mess, it is necessary to get your own hands dirty."

"Of what do you speak? You talk of seeing the Countess Mircalla," exclaimed my father, incredulously. "Why, she has been dead more than a century!"

"Not as dead as you fancy, I am told," answered the General.

"I confess, General, you puzzle me utterly!" replied my father, looking at him, I fancied, for a moment with a return of the suspicion I detected before. But although there was anger and detestation at times in the General's manner, there was nothing flighty.

"There remains to me," he said, as we passed under the heavy arch of the Gothic church—for its dimensions would have justified its being so styled—"but one object which can interest me during the years that remain to me on earth, and that is to wreak on her the vengeance which, I thank God, may still be accomplished by a mortal arm."

"What vengeance can you mean?" asked my father, in increasing amazement.

"I mean to decapitate the monster!" he answered, with a fierce flush and a stamp that echoed mournfully through the hollow ruin, his clenched hand was at the same moment raised, as if it grasped the handle of an axe, while he shook it ferociously in the air.

"What?" exclaimed my father, more than ever bewildered.

"I intend to strike off her head!"

"Cut off her head?"

"Aye, with a hatchet, a spade, or anything that can cleave through her murderous throat. You shall listen and then understand," he answered, trembling with rage. And hurrying forward he said: "That beam will answer for a seat; your dear child is fatigued. Let her be seated, and I will in a few sentences close my dreadful story."

The squared block of wood, which lay on the grass-grown pavement of the chapel, formed a bench on which I was very glad to rest myself. In the meantime, the General called to the woodman, who had been removing some boughs which leaned upon the old walls, and, axe in hand, the hardy old fellow stood before us.

He could not tell us anything of these monuments; but there were two men he said, one a nobleman, the other a doctor, at present sojourning in the house of the priest, about two miles away. According to his wife, who kept house for the priest, she had overheard the trio discussing these very ruins, and the two visitors seemed very knowledgeable about this place. It was possible, from what his wife had told him, the nobleman could likely point out every monument of the old Karnstein family. Also, for a trifle, if we were so inclined he would undertake to bring them back with him, if we would lend him one of our horses, for little more than half an hour.

I noted, as did my father, that the General nodded his head knowingly at mention of the two strangers, although he offered no further insight into them.

"Have you been long employed about this forest?" asked my father of the old man.

"I have been a woodman here," he answered in his patois, "under the forester, all my days; so has my father before me, and so on, as many generations as I can count up. I could show you the very house in the village here, in which my ancestors lived."

"How came the village to be deserted?" asked the General.

"It was troubled by revenants, sir, it was long ago, but nonetheless it was a true event. Several of the fiends were tracked to their graves, there detected by the usual tests, and extinguished in the usual way, by decapitation, the stake, or burning; but not until many of the villagers were killed."

I nudged my father gently in his ribs, "What's a revenant?" I whispered.

"Hush child," snapped my father, expressing a surprisingly stern countenance.

"Even after all these proceedings, which were conducted according to the old laws," continued the man—"so many graves opened, and so many vampires deprived of their horrible animation—the village was not relieved. But a Moravian nobleman, who happened to be travelling this way, heard how matters were, and being skilled—as many people were in his country—in such affairs, he offered to deliver the village from its tormentor. He did so in this way: There was a bright moon that night, and he ascended, shortly after sunset, the towers of the chapel here, from whence he could distinctly see the churchyard beneath him. You can see it from that window. From this point he watched until he saw the vampire come out of his grave, and place near it the linen clothes in which he had been folded and laid to rest. The nobleman then observed as the revenant glided away towards the village to plague its inhabitants.

"The stranger, having seen all this, came down from the steeple, took the linen wrappings of the vampire, and carried them back up to the top of the tower, which he once again mounted. When the vampire returned from his prowling and missed his clothes, he cried furiously to the Moravian, whom he saw at the summit of the tower, and who, in reply, beckoned him to ascend and take them. Whereupon the vampire, accepting his invitation, began to climb the steeple, and as soon as he had reached the battlements, the Moravian, with a stroke of his sword, clove his skull in two, hurling him down to the churchyard, whither. Descending by the winding stairs, the stranger followed and cut his head clean off, and next day delivered it and the body to the villagers, who duly impaled and burnt them.

"This Moravian nobleman had authority from the then head of the family to remove the tomb of Mircalla, Countess Karnstein, lest any lingering force of evil should seek redress, by inflicting itself upon the lineage of this noble family. He carried out his task effectually, so that in a little while its site was quite forgotten."

"Can you point out where it stood?" asked the General, eagerly.

The forester shook his head, and smiled.

"Not a living soul could tell you that now," he said. "Besides, although it is said that her body was removed; no one can be sure of that either."

Having thus spoken, and as time pressed, we bade him well. He then dropped his axe, and accompanied by Madame, who was to instruct our coachman to unhitch a horse, departed towards our carriage, leaving us to hear the remainder of the General's strange story.

Chapter 22

Correspondence from Laura Bennett, addressed to Doctor Hesselius. *March 24th, 1871*

"My beloved Bertha," the General resumed, "was now growing rapidly worse. The physician who attended her had failed to produce the slightest impression on her disease, for such I then supposed it to be. He saw my alarm and suggested a consultation. I called in an abler physician from Gratz.

"Several days elapsed before he arrived. He was a good and pious, as well as a learned man. Having seen my poor darling together, they withdrew to my library to confer and discuss. I, from the adjoining room where I awaited their summons, heard these two gentlemen's voices raised in something sharper than a strictly philosophical discussion. I knocked at the door and entered. I found the physician from Gratz maintaining his theory. His rival was combating it with undisguised ridicule, accompanied with bursts of laughter. This unseemly manifestation subsided and the altercation ended on my entrance.

"'Sir,' said my first physician, 'my learned brother seems to think that you require a conjuror, and not a doctor.'

"'Pardon me,' said the older physician, from Gratz, looking displeased, 'I shall state my own view of the case in my own way another time. I grieve, Monsieur le General, that by my skill and science I can be of no use. Before I go I shall do myself the honour to suggest something to you.'

"He seemed thoughtful, and sat down at a table and began to write. Profoundly disappointed, I made my bow, and as I turned to go, the other doctor pointed over his shoulder to his companion who was writing, and then, with a shrug, significantly touched his forehead.

"This consultation then, left me precisely where I was. I walked out into the grounds, all but distracted. The doctor from Gratz, in ten or fifteen minutes, overtook me. He apologized for having followed me, but said that he could not conscientiously take his leave without a few words more. He told me that he had read of many such cases and could not be mistaken; no natural disease exhibited the same symptoms; and that in all likelihood death was already very near. There remained however, a day or possibly two, of life. If the fatal seizure were at once arrested, with great care and skill her strength might possibly return. But all hung now upon the confines of the irrevocable. One more assault might extinguish the last spark of vitality which is, every moment, ready to fade and die.

"'And what is the nature of the seizure you speak of?' I entreated.

"'I have stated all fully in this note, which I place in your hands upon the distinct condition that you send for the nearest clergyman and open my letter in his presence, on no account read it till he is with you; you would despise it else, and it is a matter of life and death. Should the priest fail you, then indeed you may read it.'

"He then asked me, before taking his leave finally, whether I would wish to see a man curiously learned upon the very subject, who, after I had read his letter, would probably interest me above all others, and he urged me earnestly to invite him to visit him there; and so took his leave.

"The ecclesiastic was absent, and I read the letter by myself. At another time, or in another case, it might have excited my ridicule. But into what quackeries will not people rush for a last chance, where all accustomed means have failed, and the life of a beloved object is at stake?

"Nothing, you will say, could be more absurd than the learned man's letter. It was monstrous enough to have consigned him to a madhouse. He said that although his experience of such things was limited, he believed, based upon written works he had studied, that the patient was suffering from the visits of a vampire! The punctures which she described as having occurred near the throat, were, he insisted, the insertion of those two long, thin, and sharp teeth which, it is well known are peculiar to vampires; and there could be no doubt, he added, as to the well-defined presence of the small livid mark which all concurred in describing as that induced by the demon's lips, and every symptom described by the sufferer was in exact conformity with those recorded in every case of a similar visitation.

"Once, as you who know me might well imagine, I myself would have been wholly sceptical as to the existence of any such portent as the vampire. But even by then, at the time of this occurrence, I was no longer the man you have known for years. Without dwelling unduly upon my reasoning, other than to say that surely misery and desperation both played their part in forcing my hand, I was at such a loss, that rather than try nothing, I acted upon the instructions of the letter.

"I concealed myself in the dark dressing room, which opens into poor Bertha's restroom, in which a candle was burning, and watched there till she was fast asleep. I stood at the door, peeping through the small crevice. My sword lay on the table beside me, as my directions prescribed. A little after one, I saw a large black object; very ill-defined, crawl, as it seemed to me, up onto the bed. It swiftly spread itself up to the poor girl's throat, where it swelled, in a moment, into a great palpitating mass.

"For a few moments I had stood petrified. I now sprang forward, with my sword in my hand. The black creature suddenly contracted towards the foot of the bed, glided over it, and, standing on the floor about a yard clear of the bed, with a glare of skulking ferocity and horror fixed on me, I saw Millarca.

Speculating I know not what, I struck at her instantly with my sword; but already she was gone. I turned, just in time to see her standing near the door, unscathed. Horrified, I pursued and struck again. Again, she was gone; and my sword flew to shivers against the door.

"I can't describe to you all that passed on that horrible night. The whole house was up and stirring. The spectre Millarca was gone. But her victim was sinking fast, and before the morning dawned, she died."

The General was agitated. We did not speak to him. My father, trailed by our manservant, walked a short distance and began reading the inscriptions on the tombstones; and thus occupied, he strolled into the door of a side chapel to prosecute his researches. The General leaned against the wall, dried his eyes, and sighed heavily. I was relieved on hearing the voices of Carmilla and Madame, who were at that moment approaching. The voices died away.

In this solitude, having just listened to so strange a story, connected, as it was, with the great and titled dead, whose monuments were mouldering among the dust and ivy surrounding us, and every incident of which bore so awfully upon my own mysterious case—in this haunted spot, darkened by the towering foliage that rose on every side, dense and high above its noiseless walls—a horror began to steal over me, and my heart sank as I thought that my friends were, after all, not about to enter and disturb this triste and ominous scene.

The General's eyes were fixed on the ground, as he leaned with his hand upon the basement of a shattered monument.

Under a narrow, arched doorway, surmounted by one of those demoniacal grotesques in which the cynical and ghastly fancy of old Gothic carving delights, I saw very gladly the beautiful face and figure of Carmilla enter the shadowy chapel.

I was just about to rise and speak, and nodded smiling, in answer to her peculiarly engaging smile; when with a cry, the old soldier by my side caught up the woodman's hatchet, which had been discarded on the ground, and started forward. On seeing him, a brutalized change came over Carmilla's features. It was an instantaneous and horrible transformation, as she made a crouching step backwards. Before I could utter a scream, he struck at her with all his force, but she dived under his blow, and unscathed, caught him in her tiny grasp by the wrist. He struggled for a moment to release his arm, and then screamed as the frail girl tightened her grip; a sickening crunching sound filling the air as the bones in his wrist shattered beyond repair. The General's hand opened, the axe falling to the ground with an almighty clang, and the General, still tightly locked in Carmilla's grip, sank to his knees. Carmilla raised her open hand, bony fingers spread wide, claw like, and ready to strike out at the stricken man kneeling before her. I remember screaming in disbelief at the events unfolding before my eyes, and then screaming again, this time at Carmilla, urging her that she should stop! Then as she turned and looked in my direction, for the first time, I saw the change that had overtaken her.

Carmilla's hair no longer shone with the vitality of life, it was dull and matted. Her skin too, had taken on a mottled, aged appearance. The girl's head seemed to have lengthened and her jaw hung open, almost impossibly wide, displaying two sets of needle sharp teeth. But worst of all were her eyes. I had never before seen a dead person; even so, as I looked into those cold black eyes, I was sure they would have more befitted a corpse.

Carmilla turned her attention back upon the General; once more raising her hand, intent on striking what I was sure would be a disastrous blow. She emitted a cry of such rage; I was forced to stop my fingers in my ears as it echoed around the ruined chapel. I winced, and for a second, time seemed to stand still as I contemplated what I might do to assist the General, and to free my friend for whom I felt such affection, from the demon that had surely possessed her.

However, my musing was short lived. I heard it first, snarling like a roar of thunder. Then I saw him, the General's companion, tearing off his shirt as he ran, moving at speed through the chapel, moving far more swiftly than should ever have been possible.

He was within twenty paces of Carmilla before I even realised the change which had overtaken him. He had now lost his shirt, and I could see that his body was covered in thick brisling hairs. His jaw had lengthened, and the features now more closely resembled those of a wolf, rather than that of a man. During the transformation, the bandage had fallen away from the thing's face, revealing an area of horrendous scarring. I noted too that one of the creature's ears had been torn off, and could only assume that sometime previously the beast itself had been the victim of a most hideous assault. I noticed also that this creature, for certainly it was no longer a man, had grown during the transformation. It had, by my own estimation, grown several inches in stature, and maybe as much as doubled its bodyweight.

The beast launched itself into the air, intent on striking a fatal blow at Carmilla's throat. She was able to avoid its leap, and using her arms to parry the creature, she succeeded in sending it crashing into one of the ancient pews, which shattered beneath its weight. Although in doing so she was forced to release her hold on the General, who sank limply to the ground.

After watching the beast's less than elegant landing, I turned once more to Carmilla. She glanced briefly at the stricken general lying at her feet, then once more towards me, and then she was gone.

I like to think that, at least for that moment, even if only for an instant, her features softened, becoming more like those of the beautiful young woman who had forever found a place within my heart. Although my momentary daydream was all too quickly disturbed, first by the harrowed cry of my father, and then by the sound of a musket being discharged.

Looking up, I was horrified to see the wolf-man bearing down on me. Except that there was no longer anything of the *man* to be seen. The creature had succeeded in removing the last vestige of its garments, and now, transformation complete, presented itself as a huge grey wolf. I did not know at the time, but the gunshot I heard was the vain attempt of our manservant to *down* the beast, before it could reach me. Although I remained at a loss as to why I should have presented a target for the furious creature. Unfortunately, and probably understandable too given the nature of the situation, our servant's aim proved not to be true on this day. At the very last moment, just as the creature was about to vent itself upon me, I closed my eyes. I had no wish to look death in the face.

The whole frightful scene had passed in barely moments, although I am sure you will indulge me, when I say that for me those were the longest moments of my life.

Chapter 23

Correspondence from Laura Bennett, addressed to Doctor Hesselius. *March 6th, 1871*

Obviously, I had survived the best efforts of the beast, or else doubtless I would not be entering into correspondence with you now.

The first thing I recollect is opening my eyes, only to find myself lying on the ground, Papa and Madame kneeling beside me. Papa was holding my hand and gently stroking my hair, while Madame was impatiently repeating again and again, the question, "Where is Mademoiselle Carmilla?"

I answered numbly, "I don't know—I can't tell—she went there, I think," and I pointed, limply, to the door through which Madame had presumably just entered.

"But I have been standing there in the passage, ever since Mademoiselle Carmilla entered; and she did not return."

"Hush now, Madame," urged my father, gently gripping her forearm. "Try to stay calm."

"Stay calm, how on earth am I to stay calm? Look at this place, it is desolation. People are dead, and dying, and Mademoiselle Carmilla is once again missing!"

It was obvious to me that the usually staid Madame was in a state of shock. Though I suspect no more so than was I, given that I was able to sustain a remarkable degree of calm. Surprisingly so, when taking into account the events I had witnessed.

Madame then edged herself free from my father's grip, and rising to her feet she walked slowly away, calling "Carmilla!"

Father instructed the servant with the axe to trail Madame, which he did as she then repeated the call through every door and passage and from the windows, but no answer came.

It was only as my father first began talking with the servant, I realised that the chapel had become a veritable hive of activity. Many men, all of them bearing arms, were moving hastily throughout the chapel, carrying out searches of the alcoves and vestries. Intent, as I was sure they were, on finding Carmilla and freeing her from the clutches of whatever demon now possessed her. In the centre of the aisle stood a man whose vestments seemed to indicate high office, although he was surely one of the strangest looking men I have ever beheld. He was tall, narrow-chested, stooping, but with high shoulders. His face was brown and dried in with deep furrows; he wore an oddly-shaped hat with a broad leaf. His hair, long and grizzled, hung on his shoulders. He wore a pair of gold spectacles, and seemed to wear a perpetual half-smile; his long thin arms were gesticulating widely, and his lank hands, in old black gloves ever so much too wide for them, waved and gestured instructions to the searching militia. Over by the font, a priest, hands clasped together, as though in prayer, was in deep conversation with the old woodman.

I endeavoured to sit up, but Papa insisted I remain rested, at least until the doctor had examined me. As he mentioned the doctor, Papa had given the slightest of motions towards the overturned pew away to my left. I turned my head, in response to his gesture, and was immediately struck with horror. Barely twenty paces from me, on the chapel floor, lay the prone body of a naked man. Both the copious amounts of blood and the woodman's axe, deeply imbedded in the side of the man's skull, confirmed that he was beyond any medical assistance.

The scene of horror with which I was now confronted unfortunately proved not to be the finale. Just a short distance from the dead man, his back propped against the broken pew, into which the wolf-creature had earlier been sent mercilessly crashing, was the General. Even from my own position it was obvious to see that his injuries were most severe. He was being tended by another man, who I recognised immediately as Doctor Alvinci, the physician who had earlier visited with us.

Despite my protestations, Papa insisted I remain where I was, although he did at least allow me the dignity of sitting up. Shortly, Mademoiselle De Lafontaine appeared, being trailed by one of the armed militia. He informed my father that, although not a trained physician, he had acted as a field medic during his time in the Royal Army.

My father said that he was satisfied for the man to assess my condition, given his previous experience, so long as this was acceptable for me too. Naturally I was in agreement, and in just a short time I had been given an *almost* clean bill of health. Somewhat embarrassingly, it turned out that when the wolf had launched itself towards me, I had fainted with fright. Thus the only wound inflicted upon me was a very large bump on the back of my head, which was sustained as I fell to the floor.

Upon regaining my composure, Father and I moved over to where the General lay. As it had transpired, the General had saved my life, but had been critically wounded in doing so. As the werewolf, for that is most assuredly what it was, launched its attack upon me, the General had picked up the woodman's axe and selflessly flung himself at the creature. The old soldier had emerged victorious from the ensuing melee, but at grave cost to himself. The beast's teeth had pierced his chest, inflicting a deep wound.

We stood solemnly, for what seemed an eternity; tears welled in my eyes as Doctor Alvinci battled to stem the loss of blood. I could tell from the faces of those others who gathered around, the outcome was not anticipated to be a satisfactory one. But eventually, under the skilled hands of the good doctor, the wound was forced to yield its advantage. Doctor Alvinci, shirt sleeves rolled high and forearms covered in blood, looked to the gathered throng, and spoke.

"That's it; I have succeeded in stopping the outflow of blood. It is in God's hands now as to whether the General has the strength left to win this battle."

As he finished speaking, General Spielsdorf slowly opened his eyes, raised his head just slightly, and gestured for the doctor to move closer. The General then spent some minutes whispering into the doctor's ear, and as he did so the doctor's countenance grew graver by the moment.

When the General had finished talking, he closed his eyes and sank back into unconsciousness. Doctor Alvinci rose to his feet, and asked that both the priest and my father join him and the nobleman, whom he referred to as Baron Vordenburg, in private conversation.

The four men then walked off into one of the far vestries, closing the door behind them.

While we were waiting for them to reappear, a number of the militia constructed a makeshift stretcher on which to place the General.

Madame and I were still busily wondering as to the nature of the information the General had supplied, when the vestry door opened and all four men, looking exceedingly grim, reappeared.

Papa approached, and instructed that Madame, Mademoiselle De Lafontaine, and I would not be returning home this evening. Instead, we were to be accompanied under armed escort back to

Father Wagner's house. I protested loudly, insisting on returning to our schloss, lest Carmilla had returned and required our assistance.

Papa though, denied my protestations, and would be drawn no further as to why we could not return home, other than to say, "There is much evil afoot this day. I have complete faith that these fine men are more than qualified in dispatching such matters, but until such time as they do, I need to be certain in my own mind that you fine ladies remain safe. Believe me when I say to you, knowing that you are under the care of Father Wagner will offer me great peace of mind. There is much to do, and in order that I can give my fullest attention to a most pressing matter, first I must know that you ladies remain safe."

"But what of Carmilla?" I insisted.

"Do not let it trouble you about Carmilla," answered my father, "most assuredly, we will find her."

My father's words failed to satisfy me. I needed to return home, in the hope that I might find Carmilla safe and well, and free from the clutches of the demon that had possessed her.

Despite my protestations, Papa insisted the ladies and I join the party headed for the priest's house, and so with an armed escort of four militia men, we set off for Father Wagner's home. As we left, I couldn't help but notice the look of grim concern upon the face of my father.

Chapter 24

Excerpt from the journal of Doctor Alvinci, *September 4th, 1860*

"They are all wolves!" That sentence shall haunt me, and send a chill creeping down my spine for the rest of my days. Those were the words whispered to me by General Spielsdorf, as he lay injured on the floor of the old Karnstein chapel, amid a scene of mayhem and devastation.

It is only right that a record of these events, which have occurred, is set down for posterity, lest in the minds of future generations such things are dismissed into the realm of folklore and fable.

I write these words now from the home of Thomas Bennett, the Englishman who lives with his daughter, Laura, in a schloss barely three miles east of the Karnstein ruins. We made our return to the Bennett home almost three hours ago, after arranging for Laura, and two other ladies of the house, to be placed into the care of Father Wagner.

Already it has proven to be a most eventful evening. This, in turn follows on from what has been a most remarkable day, although not, I fear, one without dire consequence.

The General Spielsdorf, for all of my efforts, is unlikely to see out the night. His wound is deep, and he suffers untold internal damage.

Thankfully, upon our return he did regain consciousness, at least for a short while, and I was further able to question him regarding the nature of what has occurred. I have done all I can for him now, and his fate is very much in God's hands. The General's own hands are far from clean regarding much that has taken place these past days, but without doubt, his selfless actions earlier today most assuredly served to save the life of young Laura Bennett.

It pains me that I can do no more for the General, seeing as I feel so deeply that I failed the man once before, for it was upon my advice that he hid in a side room, next to his betrothed's bedroom. If only though I had made a stronger case, I may have been better able to convince him of the danger his loved one faced. Then he would not have attempted to apprehend the fiend alone. Mayhap, the revenant would have been dispatched, and his precious Bertha might yet have lived. All of this though, it is just wild speculation, questions for which there can be no answers. Indeed, the past hours have offered up much cause for further contemplation.

Earlier today, Father Wagner, the Baron and I, along with our escort, were mounted and ready to leave for the Karnstein ruins, when we spied a rider approaching us with haste. We had hoped he may have been carrying dispatches which the Baron had formally requested, unfortunately those papers failed to arrive, and the horseman was an old fellow who works within the woods.

The old woodman informed us that a party of strangers were at the Karnstein ruins, and seemed intent on finding the tomb of Mircalla, Countess Karnstein. I had earlier informed Baron Vordenburg that I was prior acquainted with General Spielsdorf, and had already given him my account of the events surrounding the final days of Bertha Rheinfeldt. He in turn had informed me that the General, who was a man he trusted and had known well over a number of years, had become convinced that the fiend responsible for the murder of his betrothed was in some way linked to the old legends surrounding the Karnstein family.

We realised immediately that it must have been the General who was at the ruins, as the Baron had sent a dispatch urging him to meet with us, and on this very day.

So our party set off at pace, we ourselves being somewhat at a loss due to the old maps and papers relating to the Karnstein family, which the Baron had been awaiting delivery of, and which had so far failed to arrive. Hence, somewhat nullifying our usefulness in the hunt for any hidden chambers within the ruins. Chambers wherein, the Baron suspected, revenants may have been lurking.

We were eager to reach the archaic place, hopeful that the General's labours may have proven more fruitful. Upon our arrival, we were greeted by a scene of carnage.

The facts, garnered from those who witnessed the events unfold, including the General himself, are as follows.

Following on from the murder of Bertha Rheinfeldt, General Spielsdorf took the understandable decision to track down and destroy the vampiric fiend responsible. Where the situation became more bizarre is that the General, a man who, although retired from military service, could still I am sure garner substantial military assistance, instead made the decision to enlist the services of a pack of werewolves, in order that he might hunt down and put an end to the revenant, which he so desperately sought.

I do not know which is odder. That he would choose to make a pact with such strange beasts of myth, or indeed that he was able to actually find and enlist the services of such vile creatures of destruction.

According to the General, the deaths that have occurred locally, which have been attributable to the wolves, have all involved those people whom revenants have fed upon, and would therefore too soon become the walking dead. The werewolves have been able to detect the *stench of death,* which these souls had been cursed with, and accordingly have wrecked destruction upon them. The decapitation, and scattering of their body parts, is further ritual aimed at denying them a vampire existence.

When Carmilla, the young lady who had been staying under the care of the Bennett family, entered the chapel, the General recognised her immediately as the woman known to him as Millarca.

"She called herself Carmilla?" asked the General, agitated, as I earlier explained to him that Millarca and Carmilla were one and the same.

"Carmilla, yes," I answered. "That is the name she is known by to the Bennett family."

I then told him the story, as it had been explained to me, of how Carmilla's carriage had overturned, and her mother had then sought the assistance of Thomas Bennett in caring for her daughter,

"Aye," he had said; "that was Millarca. And that is the same person who long ago was called Mircalla, Countess Karnstein. I fear that her evil has already touched this schloss. That is why Karl, my young companion, who had transformed into a wolf, attempted to attack Laura. I had already noted the girl's lack of vigour, although hadn't pondered that she too may have been the victim of a vampire. Karl would have sensed its presence about her, as would his brothers, hence the reason that I asked you to send her away, for her own safety."

"How can you be so sure about any of this?" I had asked.

Before the General had a chance to reply, Baron Vordenburg, who had been standing behind me quietly conversing with Herr Bennett, proceeded to step forward, and pronounced loudly, "I believe the General to be correct in his assertions."

He then went on to explain how he had previous experience of a werewolf clan. Some twenty years earlier in the Northern Territory, twenty werewolves; all members of the same family, had conducted a reign of terror after one of their number was hunted down and killed.

They had systematically tracked down and killed every family member of those involved with the initial killing of their kin. Their senses were so keen; they could literally smell that people were related. The Royal Army was sent in to dispatch the beasts, but the creatures were so formidable that in the end a bargain had to be struck. The murders they had committed would be expunged from the record book, on condition they left the territories that very day, never to return.

That was why, explained the Baron, that following on from the earlier incident at the ruins, he had instructed two of his militia men to carry away the body of the young werewolf, and dispose of him in the lime pits outside of Gratz. Thus denying his werewolf kin access to the body, and hence, knowledge of the General's involvement in his death.

The Baron had heard the General's other travelling companions were waiting at the schloss, and had deduced that they too might be werewolves, as these creatures tended to move in packs. He instructed that prior to our returning to the Bennett home, I dress the General's wounds in such a way so as not be apparent a wolf had caused them. After I had done this, he doused the General's clothing with a bottle of Sal Volatile. Furthermore, he had insisted that we concoct a version of events with which to satisfy the half dozen waiting men, so they would believe that the oupire, whom they sought, had attacked and injured the General, and their young compatriot had thereafter set off in pursuit of the revenant, but had then failed to return.

Upon our return to the schloss, we had shared *our* version of the happenings at Karnstein, with the waiting men. They made haste to leave immediately, informing us they would return once they had recovered their brother. They left on foot; they would not be fast enough to catch the two militia men.

We had not at the time known why the Baron had insisted on these constraints, regarding the information to be shared with the General's men. Now though, all was becoming clear.

It transpired the documents and maps, which the Baron had been waiting for, contained information pertaining to the burial sites at Karnstein, but specifically the hidden tomb of Mircalla, Countess Karnstein. The Baron asserted that he believed General Spielsdorf to be correct in assuming that Mircalla, or whichever name she was now using, was indeed the centre for the evil plaguing this district. He showed us a map, on which he had plotted all known suspected cases of vampirism, within a forty mile radius, and having taken place within the last ten years. At the centre of the web was Karnstein Castle.

The Baron has dispatched a rider to collect the maps we need. Within two days we shall have the information we require. We will then be ready to do away with this most Bloody Countess.

While the Baron was making his acknowledgements, General Spielsdorf slipped into a deep state of unconsciousness. I fear the next twenty four hours will be critical.

Herr Bennett stayed silent for much of the time. He had vented his fury at the General's actions when we talked earlier, in the vestry. He could not believe that a man he considered one of his oldest friends, would endanger his loved ones so, by allowing a band of *werewolves* to travel to, and enter into his home. I fear that even if a miracle was to occur, and the General should somehow manage a recovery, this is a friendship that is now spent.

Chapter 25

Excerpt from the private journal of General Spielsdorf, *September 6th, 1860*

I awakened to the sound of horses being readied, down in the courtyard. I listened intently as what seemed a multitude of men busied themselves. The smell of nervous anticipation among the men and the horses was palpable in the morning air.

I realised what was happening, even before Baron Vordenburg knocked on my door, sometime later.

I bid him enter, and as he did so the look of surprise upon his face was obvious. Even though, I am sure, Doctor Alvinci had already made announcements as to my miraculous recovery.

My old friend, Thomas, has barely been able to look me in the eye. I know he is filled with what he feels to be a righteous anger. He readily expressed his dismay, regarding my 'having entered into a pact with those creatures of Satan.'

Pray that I were willing to share the truth with him, regarding my ties with these *wolf-men*. I truly believe though, such a truth would only further his disdain for me. Thomas is a man of staid character, which does not lend itself to ready acceptance of the wondrous.

It has been less than two full days since my encounter with Mircalla, Countess Karnstein, and the somewhat unfortunate killing of Karl Rheinfeldt, which followed. It is an action of which I am deeply regretful. But I could not allow the boy to turn his rage on Laura Bennett, even if she has been afflicted with the same evil which doomed his sister.

Poor Bertha, so many times she had passed comment, likening the feelings aroused in her by the woman we knew as Millarca, to those of being around *family*. But I refuse to accept that she bore any semblance of nature akin to that fiend. I just wish the both of us had been able to realise what a foul creature it was we unwittingly invited into our home.

As for myself, I begin to suspect that my tussle with the boy may serve to have long term consequences. The wolf had bitten deeply into my chest and for sure I should have bled out, were it not for the timely intervention of the good Doctor Alvinci. Yet already the wound has begun to heal, to the degree that it no longer pains me. My wrist too, which was shattered by the she fiend, although still fitted with a splint, I am easily able to write in this journal.

My powers of recovery would seem to be functioning at the maxim, as are my other senses too. I sit here now listening, not only to the birds singing in the trees, but also to the fluttering wings of a butterfly, which moments ago passed by my window.

In the corridor, a servant has just passed by my door; my senses inform me the girl is experiencing menstruation.

Further away still, I can smell rabbits being skinned down in the kitchens.

There can be little doubt; a change is fast overtaking me. It is one that Bertha had once alluded to. Pray she was here now, that she might share this awakening with me.

I cannot believe it has been but two years, since I found the woman who would forever change my life. Sharp is the agony, to find such a love only to then have it stolen away again.

I remember it well, how it first began.

Journeying alone, I had almost a week earlier travelled out to the western forests, some forty miles from my schloss.

It is an area I first visited when I was just a boy; on what was to be my first hunting expedition. Father had taken the decision to make it an experience that I would long remember.

Our party travelled deep into the forest, until we arrived at an old lodge, which my father's men had constructed many years previously.

We spent two weeks there that first time, hunting with bows, as my father always felt this presented more of a challenge. It was a challenge I revelled in.

Father, as is the norm amongst the males of our family, was a military man, and the time we spent together was scarce. To get those two weeks, uninterrupted by his being called back to barracks, for me, it was like a gift from heaven.

We made many return journeys to the lodge.

After his death, I chose to continue the tradition. Even during my service in the Royal Army, at least once every year, more often when able; I would journey by myself to the wilderness.

My working life consisted of being surrounded by, and barking out orders to commissioned men, hence, any opportunity for solace was something to be relished. The lodge, with the good memories it held for me, was my perfect haven.

Strangely, for someone who has enjoyed a life in the army, I have always found that when given the choice, I have been happiest in my own company. Or at least that is how I had always felt, before that day when everything in my life changed.

It was late afternoon, and I had spent a number of hours tracking a wounded stag on foot. My earlier shot having narrowly missed the creature's heart.

I had been forced to set loose my horse, this part of the forest becoming too dense for a mount, but the steed was one I had owned for years, and I had faith it would return safely to the lodge.

Now though, silent as death, and given cover by a rotting hulk of felled oak, I finally had the animal in my sight. It was no longer about the hunt. All I was concerned with now was showing the creature some compassion. If I didn't make the shot it could take several more hours for the deer to bleed out. I pulled back the bow string and said a silent prayer, wishing the animal a speedy journey into the next life.

That was when I saw her, the she-wolf, moving slowly through the long grass, intent on staking a claim on the injured deer. I slackened off my bow string, watching transfixed as the sleek animal moved in for the kill. The stag had travelled too far for me to make use of its carcass. Better then, I thought, to let the wolf have its fill of a hearty meal.

The creature was magnificent. I had never seen a white wolf before, and for a moment I considered taking my shot. I should certainly have garnered a most prized pelt.

However, I quickly relented. Such a beautiful animal as this did not deserve to end its days on the point of my arrow.

The wolf was not long in making its attack. Having closed the distance quickly it was fast upon the deer; its leap carried it fully onto the stags back, an attempt to drag its already injured prey to ground. The deer had already looked unsteady on its legs and it breathed with a horrible wheezing sound. Blood was flooding into its lungs as a result of the damage caused by my earlier arrow. Even so, the stag was now in a fight for his life, and he would not give up the battle easily.

More by luck than judgement the deer spun around, and in doing so was able to unseat its unwelcome rider, immediately taking the opportunity to gore the downed beast. Its large antlers pierced the floored wolf's shoulder, and the animal let out a howl of indignation and pain. Quickly, the wolf regained its footing, and its second strike saw it lock onto the deer's hind legs. As the stag crashed to the ground, the white wolf switched its attack once more. This time it latched onto the stag's throat. Just once, the deer made a bleating sound, but then it was done.

I watched silently as the injured wolf ate its fill. Once again I contemplated putting an arrow in the animal, this time reasoning that it may die anyway as a result of the goring it had received. But injured or not, I had no wish to end this magnificent creature, and so I silently wished it well, and then watched as it finished its meal, before limping off into the forest.

I took a few cuts of meat from the dead deer, and then set off at a steady pace, back in the direction of the lodge.

During my hunt I had traversed the edge of Boer Lake, a vast expanse of open water, nestled within the depths of the forest. Even through the canopy of the trees, the afternoon sun was high overhead, and I decided to stop off and bathe in the waters of the lake.

As I stepped out from the tree line, I saw a figure down by the bank, silhouetted against the sun-gilded waters. I stopped in my tracks, as I realised it was a young woman, bereft of clothes, washing herself in the cool water.

The woman started as she realized my presence. Jumping to her feet, she began backing off into the water. I called out that I meant her no harm, and began stepping forward towards her, confused as to who she might be, as I knew this place well and there were no locals living this deeply in the forest.

As I closed the distance, I noticed that the woman's shoulder was bleeding. Closer still, I could see that she carried a deep wound that was in dire need of dressing.

She had stopped retreating from me, now she just stood silently, waist deep in the water. I called out to her, once again reiterating that I meant her no harm. She opened her mouth, so as to speak, but the words never left her lips. Instead, the effects of her injury caught up with her, consciousness slipped away and she dropped like a stone, disappearing beneath the surface of the lake.

I waded into the water, dragging her clear, and laying her gently down on the grass bank.

I was in awe, the girl was barely half my age, but without doubt she was the most exquisite creature I had ever laid eyes on.

She was small in stature, but with a perfectly proportioned figure, all of which was available to see before my eyes. Her hair was white blonde and stretched halfway down her back. The girl's fingers were slender, with surprisingly long tapered nails. I was besotted.

The girl did not regain consciousness, although her breathing remained shallow but steady. I searched the banks but could find no trace of her clothing, and so, knowing that there were no other abodes in the area from which she may be missed, I took the decision to bring her back to the lodge.

She was only a slight girl, even so, we were still a league away from my dwelling, and so, after covering her modesty with my jacket, it was with some exertion that I carried her home. My hand held tightly around her shoulder as I walked; staunching the flow of blood from the nasty looking injury that she bore.

She never opened her eyes again that day. I dressed her wound, and put her to bed. By sunset the air turned cold, and so after striking the fire, I sat in the chair beside her, and remained there for the whole of the night.

I awakened in the early hours, and was surprised to find that the girl was gone. I searched the few rooms of the lodge, which were clear, and then looked outside. She was nowhere to be found.

I spent the next three days and nights puzzling over the strange girl, until finally I began to wonder if in fact the whole event hadn't all been some wild fantasy played out by my mind. The blood soaked remnants of torn cloth, with which I had cleansed her wound, served both to confirm her existence and to confound me further as to the nature of what had occurred.

As the week moved on the weather grew warmer still. I decided to head back out to Boar Lake, and spend an afternoon swimming in the crystal waters.

I tethered my mount, amid the shade of the trees, and headed towards the lake. As I passed the tree line, and stepped out onto the shoreline, a movement caught my eye.

Down by the water, silhouetted against the backdrop of a turquoise expanse, a wolf was drinking. The creature swiftly caught my scent, and holding its head high, it sniffed the air. The wolf then turned and padded softly towards me, stopping just feet away.

My hand had moved in conjunction with the wolf's approach, and was now rested on the blade holstered at my belt.

It was as the wolf moved clear of the water's glare, I recognised my old hunting partner. Standing before me, head cocked, gazing at me with unblinking, though surprisingly gentle, grey-hazel eyes, was the white she-wolf.

Time seemed transfixed, neither of us wanting, or being prepared to make a movement. Eventually, the animal moved closer, its approach now holding no fear for me, I could see from how she moved that she intended no harm.

The wolf sniffed at my fingers, before licking tenderly at the open palms of my hand. I tentatively ventured to scratch her ears, before progressing on, soon though I was running my hands through her thick glossy coat.

It would have been a bizarre and surreal sight, for anyone that had ventured our way later that day, the soldier and the she-wolf, frolicking gaily on the waters edge. We wrestled, we swam, and we chased each other around the banks. We played together like the best of friends until eventually, tired to exhaustion, we slept.

When I awoke, the wolf was gone.

I have to admit to feeling disappointed that my new friend had deserted me. Also though, a quiver of delight ran through my body. I cannot explain, but I knew our paths would cross again.

As I rode back to the cabin, my mind kept running through with the day's events. Wolves just didn't interact with man in this way. Maybe the animal was partly tamed? Perhaps a hunter had killed a she-wolf and then raised her orphaned cub. Yes, that was likely the truth of it.

Reaching the lodge, I was startled to find an open door.

Smoke was rising from the chimney, someone had struck a fire.

Had another hunter seen the cabin while passing, and decided to investigate? Dismounting, I approached cautiously, my fingers wrapped tightly around my drawn blade.

The girl lay curled on a bearskin rug in front of the fireplace. Her white blonde hair contrasted against the fresh pink of her naked skin. She supported her chin with her hands, watching my approach with wide wary eyes.

I just stared. I was so relieved to see her again, and yet my mind was racing to understand the situation.

"Who are you?" I asked at last.

She did not answer. Her expression was something of a wolfish grin. I felt a hot flush colour my cheeks. Picking up a spare shirt, I flung it to the girl.

"Put it on, young lady!" I ordered.

Her face sobered, she regarded the garment for a moment, before swinging her gaze back to me.

"You should cover yourself!" I insisted.

The girl remained silent. Only her eyes spoke, and as she slowly rose to her feet, their meaning was quite clear to me.

I opened my mouth to speak. I needed to know what was going on, but she had closed the distance before a single word could leave my lips. We came together, frantically, passionately, kissing, caressing, things becoming ever more frenetic, until she literally tore the shirt from off my back.

We tumbled, naked, onto the bearskin rug, the glow of the fire reflecting off her skin served only to further enhance her beauty. She gave a whimper of frustration as she fumbled wildly, in an attempt to loose me from my trousers, and then a cry as our bodies at last came together.

I awoke in the early hours, in time to see her naked form standing by the open door.

"Don't go," I urged.

She turned, and made to leave.

"What's your name? Please, I must know."

She stopped, and turned to face me. "I am not sure that I should have come here."

"Why should you not?"

"I will show you," she replied, and then she swiftly stepped out onto the veranda and proceeded down into the yard which fronts the lodge.

I followed her out, and turning to face me once more, she spoke. "My name is Bertha."

"Bertha... That is a most beautiful name."

Raising a finger to her lips she gestured me be silent, before casually dropping onto all fours. She fixed me with a wary gaze.

"If you want to see me again, then tomorrow evening leave the cabin door ajar. If you choose to leave it closed I will understand."

The change filled her with ecstasy. Rapture bubbled through her every sinew as muscles became supple, and bones realigned themselves. Her face contained a look of sensual pleasure, and not then understanding, I stepped forward, a helping hand held out before me.

I was too late, before I had even fully cleared the veranda; the white wolf was gone, carried away on swift, silent pads.

All that was left was the chill of the dawn, quickly followed by a helpless feeling of immeasurable loss.

Chapter 26

Correspondence from Laura Bennett, addressed to Doctor Hesselius. *March 26th, 1871*

The first night we ladies spent at the home of Father Wagner was a most anxious time, particularly for Madame and me. We had eaten a hearty meal, and were now sent to relaxing besides the open fire, in the priest's modest but welcoming lounge. Both Madame and I were busily worrying about the events of earlier, and in particular what had become of Carmilla. Father Wagner was attempting, somewhat vainly if I am to be honest, to allay our fears concerning Carmilla's wellbeing. Although I may venture that my own concerns were of a more personal nature than those of Madame.

Mademoiselle De Lafontaine was absent from our party. She had stepped out for some night air, with Lukas Cerny, the militia man who had tended to me earlier at the chapel.

It turned out that Lukas too had spent time in the area of the world which is referred to as the Orient, and this commonality, along with his general manner, had seemed to arouse some interest within Mademoiselle.

If it had not been that our attentions were so drawn towards Carmilla, then I dare suggest that Madame and I may have been inclined to comment more on the nature of Mademoiselle's new friendship.

As it was, we spent our time going over earlier events, and hypothesized all sorts of scenarios to account for what I had witnessed. Father Wagner, I noted, seemed somewhat reluctant to offer any possible explanations for the events which had taken place.

When the time came for us to retire for the evening, Madame informed me that, as subject to my father's instructions, she intended to sit with me while I slept. I objected, stating that it was hardly fair that Madame spend the night in a chair, while I had the comfort of a bed. My protestations fell on deaf ears.

As I snuggled down, comfortably losing myself in the fresh bedding, Madame wrapped a thick blanket across her shoulders, and settled back into a soft recliner. She had a grave look on her face as she watched Father Wagner performing a number of religious rites, at various locations within the room. I had no knowledge as to what these mutterings were meant to achieve, neither I hazard did Madame. For the both of us though, it served to bring forth unpleasant memories of the day's earlier events.

My sleep was at best fitful, and dreams of a most disturbing nature littered my period of rest.

One dream in particular, stayed with me for a long time afterwards.

I heard the voice, the one which I was accustomed to hearing since the onset of my mysterious malady. It came out of the darkness and its tone was both terrible and harsh. It said to me, "You will be mine, little darling. Your death is assured, as was mine, even before I had ever lived. Life is cruel, death is pain without pity, and you will hate me evermore. But your life is my life, and my life will be your blessing. Do not worry yourself, sweet love, for I will show you the way."

A black cloud enveloped me, and I felt pressure at the point of my previous strangulation. I panicked, and began to cry and struggle, then, just as suddenly as it began, I was relieved. I sprang up, into a sitting position, and I saw Carmilla, standing near the foot of my bed, in her finest white gown, bathed from her chin to her feet in one great stain of blood. She wore a look of sorrow upon her blood soaked face.

"I am sorry," she whispered, "but I am so long dead, and you will be dead for so long."

I wakened with a cry. Only to find that the night lights still burned brightly, and Madame still slept soundly, in the chair by the fireside. I never slept again that night.

Chapter 27

Excerpt from the private journal of General Spielsdorf, *September 6th, 1860*

The next day, following on from my encounter with the white wolf, I spent many hours trying to convince myself of another explanation for the sights I had witnessed. Maybe I had eaten some poison berries or tainted meat, or unknowingly ingested some other harmful agent, which had then impaired my functions.

The oddest thing is that I dreaded any of these circumstances should prove to elucidate the events which had occurred. The girl had made me feel alive, mayhap more alive than I ever knew to be possible.

That evening I sat waiting on the veranda, the cabin door lodged open. The sun had barely set when the wolf padded gently into the yard.

And that is how I met Bertha Rheinfeldt, the woman who I will forever adore. Of course, falling in love with a *werewolf,* for that is what she was, presented many problems. Not the least of which was her lack of social etiquette.

Bertha had been born a werewolf, raised among those of her own kind, many miles north-east of these forests. Her father had died two years ago, her mother before that, and so her brother Rudolph, became alpha male. He was the eldest of Bertha's seven brothers, and all of them were cruel and hurtful men.

A year ago Bertha decided to leave, and though the pack was angry, they granted her free will to make her own way.

Bertha said that the first time she laid eyes on me she knew there was a bond between us. I have to say, I felt the same way.

Bertha had never lived among ordinary folk, or had to dress accordingly. She had never sat down at a dining table and used fine cutlery. Neither had she ridden a horse. Nor had she ever danced the night away to the waltz, or any other musical serenade. All of these things needed to be addressed before I could unveil her as the woman I loved, and whom I intended to marry.

But understand me now; educating Bertha Rheinfeldt in the etiquette of modern life, it was never a chore. Instead it was something we made a game of, a game that we played out over several months, during which we remained, hidden away, deep within the sanctuary of the forest. And in-between Bertha's schooling, we would hunt together. Bertha would drive forth our prey, to a point where I should be waiting in ambush. All these experiences we revelled in, but nothing compared to the joy of evenings spent naked beside the open fire, holding sweet Bertha in my arms.

It all seems but a distant memory now. They are though, memories which I shall forever cherish.

After darling Bertha's death, at the hands of Millarca, or Mircalla, or whatever other damnable name the fiend chooses to use, I travelled north from my schloss. During conversation, my beloved had told me where her kin were to be found. I carried Bertha's riding hood with me; I gave it to her as a gift last Christmas, and she chose to wear it on most days. The cloak carried her scent, and for my own well being I kept it close. Knowing full well, the wolves would not attack me without first understanding my connection to their sister.

The story of our first meeting is not important, other than to say I found them a harsh and cruel bunch of fellows. Upon hearing Bertha's fate, they readily offered up their support in meting out vengeance. If I am honest though, I am not so sure they were interested in seeing justice for their kin, insomuch as relishing the opportunity for a savage hunt.

This morning, when Baron Vordenburg came to my room, to tell me a party was riding out to the ruins, intent on putting an end to the wickedness of Mircalla, Countess Karnstein, I wished him well with his hunt. He in turn promised me good news upon his return. They now had the old maps, showing the position of the Countess's tomb. Success, he assured me, was guaranteed; they would find and destroy her.

They would not.

Last night, I awakened to find a figure standing naked beside my bed. I scrambled to light the candles, and as my eyes slowly accustomed to the dark, I realised that my nocturnal caller was in fact Rudolph, the alpha male of the Rheinfeldt clan.

I do not know how long he had been there, silently observing me. I am forced to admit though; my blood ran cold as to the reasons for his unannounced calling, even more so as I spied the blood sodden sack, which he held in his hands.

Rudolph informed me the pack had tracked down their dead brother, running down the riders who had been dispatched to dispose of his corpse, within just a few short hours.

Before they died, the two militia men had told all regarding the earlier events at the chapel.

I feared in that moment that my life was to be at an end, for surely Rudolph had come to seek vengeance for the loss of his younger brother.

I was wrong.

He told me that although he would all too gladly end my days, in retribution for the violence which I had freely meted out against his sibling, he could not. The old laws forbade this. Once the dying wolf had passed forward its *gift*, the recipient was now *kin*, and therefore must be accorded due respect.

The true reason for his visitation was to inform me that our pursuit of the oupire, which had preyed on Bertha, was now at an end.

After they had recovered Karl's corpse, the pack had proceeded on to Karnstein, and there they had discovered the Countess, Mircalla.

The fiend just appeared as though spirited from behind a veil of overgrown ivy, and though at that time not certain of her true identity, they recognised the scent of death upon her, and so the pack struck as one.

They were about her before she had any chance to react, ripping and tearing at her flesh. The revenant attempted to strike back, but the weight of the assault upon her person was too heavy. Within minutes, Mircalla had been torn apart.

Rudolph opened the sack, and triumphantly pulled forth the blood soaked head and upper torso, holding all aloft as though brandishing a victory plaque. The carcass was still partly clothed in the torn remnants of a pale blue dress, which further highlighted the feminine proportions. It also made the whole scene even more unsavoury. I had wanted this *thing* dead, of that there should be no doubt, but I felt no joyous rapture at its decline.

The face had been ripped away, but I recognised still the thick brown hair, flecked with a touch of gold.

I nodded, "It is she."

Rudolph agreed that Mircalla had indeed presented as a fine woman, who carried herself well, as befitted my earlier description of her. According to Rudolph, the garments she wore, and the way she moved, was befitting of nobility. I had to hold back my scorn, what would this foul creature before me know of nobility. It was difficult for me to reconcile that this man was kin to my sweet and beautiful Bertha.

The look presented by Mircalla had denied her true nature, as is always the way with revenants, but now at last it was done.

She had been rendered into pieces, and now each of the brothers had carried away a body part. They would journey out in opposing directions, far and wide, before burning and scattering the remains, thus condemning the vampire to eternal damnation.

I was sorry that I had been denied the ending of the fiend by my own hand, although I took some solace in knowing Bertha's death had been avenged. Inside though, I am still haunted by a helpless feeling of immeasurable loss. It is a feeling I have felt but once before.

Mayhap I shall, upon my recovery, make a return to Boer Lake, and the happy memories it holds for me there.

Rudolph's final words were that I should never travel northwards again. The pack was returning to the hinterland. The old law may forbid any act of retribution against me, but if I ever again chose to venture into their territory, then they in turn might choose to forgo the old ways.

It was indeed a stark warning, and one to which I intend to pay the strictest heed.

Without further words, Rudolph turned toward the open window, and was gone.

Chapter 28

Excerpt from the journal of Doctor Alvinci, *September 6th, 1860*

As we set forth from the Bennett's schloss, the mid-morning sun sat high in the sky. There was little conversation, each of us brooding over events past, and the hours forthcoming.

Our party consisted of Baron Vordenburg, six of his militia, Herr Bennett and me.

As we closed on Karnstein, I pondered just what may lie before us. I had read many antiquated books which dealt with the dispatching of revenants, all of which lead to a likely scenario of the proceedings running over and again through my mind.

Should the events have played forth in such a way as they do in literary offerings, we would have continued on to Karnstein, and there, with the help of the old maps, successfully unearthed the vampire's tomb. The grave of Mircalla, Countess Karnstein, would be opened; and Herr Bennett, the Baron, and I would recognize a perfidious though beautiful face, now disclosed to view. The features, though now over a hundred and fifty years having passed since her funeral, would remain tinted with the warmth of life. No cadaverous smell shall likely exhale from within the coffin. As the medical man, required to be present in an official capacity, I should, in all likelihood have attested the marvellous fact that there was a faint but appreciable respiration, and a corresponding action of the heart. The revenants limbs would have remained perfectly flexible, the flesh elastic; and the leaden coffin might well have been floated with blood, as much to a depth of seven inches or more the body would lay immersed.

Here then would have been all the admitted signs and proofs of vampirism. The body therefore, in accordance with ancient practice would be raised and a sharp stake driven clean through the heart of the vampire, who then shall in all probability utter a piercing shriek at said moment, in all respects such as might escape from a living person in their last agony. Then the head would be struck off, and a torrent of blood might well flow from the severed neck. The body and head should next have been placed on a pile of wood, and reduced to ashes, then to be thrown upon the river and borne away, and this territory should henceforth never again be plagued by the visits of a vampire.

The day did not proceed in any way quite as I, nor any of my compatriots envisaged.

As we arrived at the Karnstein ruins there was an unnatural quiet all around. At this time of year the forest reverberates to the mating cry of its various inhabitants. Around Karnstein the forest was still, and as silent as death.

We tied the horses, and at the Baron's behest proceeded on into the chapel. The ill feeling within the place was palpable, not helped I suspect by the scene of carnage and spilt blood, left over from our previous visit. The view that greeted our arrival was in fact far grimmer than I had previously remembered it.

Without further word, the Baron took a roll of paper from his pocket, and spread it on the worn surface of a tomb that stood by. He had a pencil case in his fingers, with which he traced imaginary lines from point to point on the paper, from there often glancing up from it and around, at certain points of the building; I concluded it to be a plan of the chapel. He accompanied his study with occasional readings from a dirty little book, whose yellow leaves were closely written over.

The Baron, closely trailed by Herr Bennett, sauntered down the side aisle, opposite to the spot where I was standing, mumbling to himself as he went. He began measuring distances by paces, and finally he stood silently facing a piece of the sidewall, a look of deep cogitation etched upon his face. He began to examine the area with great minuteness; pulling off the ivy that clung over it. The Baron pulled loose a candlestick holder free from its wall mount, and began rapping the plaster with its end, scraping here, and knocking there. At length he ascertained the existence of a broad marble tablet, with letters carved in relief upon it.

With the assistance of his men the remaining plaster was removed, revealing the disguised wall, upon which a monumental inscription, and carved escutcheon, was disclosed. They proved to be those of the long lost monument of Mircalla, Countess Karnstein.

The Baron, though not I fear given to the praying mood, raised his hands and eyes to the heavens, in mute thanksgiving for some moments.

"Now," he said; "the Inquisition will be held according to law."

The Baron's men fetched tools, which had been carried on the pack-horses, and the concealed tomb was smashed open. We all stood silently, not any one of us wishing to be the first to express our disappointment, upon our discovery that the tomb was empty.

When we arrived back at the schloss, I would venture our expressions granted us the appearance of a defeated army, returned from battle. The Baron especially, wore a huge ridge of disappointment upon his brow.

Herr Bennett and I went into the drawing room, and after sitting down and enjoying a warm mug of tea, we held a long conversation about how best to proceed.

He was adamant about two things. Firstly, and understandably, he wanted his daughter home. If Mircalla was still on the loose, then he felt better able to protect Laura from her if she was under his own roof. Even, he concluded, if it meant Father Wagner agreeing to accept his hospitality, and residing within the schloss until the situation was resolved.

Secondly, he wanted his old *friend*, General Spielsdorf, gone from within his home, and as quickly as he was able. The man was guilty of the ultimate sin, of which there could be no excuse. He had made a pact with creatures of evil, with minions of the Devil.

Losing Bertha had obviously unhinged his mind, but that could not pardon his actions with regards bringing these creatures into Herr Bennett's home.

It was more than an hour later when the Baron burst into the room, issuing instructions to a servant as he did so, to "Bring Vodka, and bring some whisky too, a celebration is in order."

Our look of surprise melted into one of pleasured relief, as the Baron informed us of how he had called upon the General, to tell him of the day's disappointments. The General, in turn, had told the Baron of the nocturnal visit of the werewolf, and of the pack's destruction of Mircalla.

The General had refrained from mentioning it earlier, because he wanted to be assured in his own mind that the vampire had indeed been destroyed. Therefore he waited until our hunting party had completed its return back from Karnstein. Furthermore, the werewolves intended to leave this area, choosing instead to return to their own hinterlands. It goes without saying, but this too is excellent news.

Later that day, I paid a visit to the General, hoping that he may choose to further elaborate, for my own benefit, as to exactly what had gone on when the werewolves confronted Mircalla. He declined, saying that, 'The matter was now done with.'

I have to say that his continued recovery continues to defy all medical logic. I would also note however, that he now has a new curtness about him, seemingly ever more discourteous and blunt.

One can only assume that the loss of his loved one has predisposed his manner so. Nonetheless, he no longer carries the warmth of character within his heart which had previously made him so appreciated.

It would seem, God willing, that this madness may finally be drawing to an end. All that is open to us for now is waiting, for surely we shall know soon enough, probably within a matter of days, if the vampire scourge has been cleansed.

As for me, these proceedings have further whetted my appetite for all things arcane. Upon my return to Gratz, I fully intend to spend my remaining years focusing on matters esoteric, in an attempt to explain the phantasmagoria that attaches itself to this world.

Chapter 29

Correspondence from Laura Bennett, addressed to Doctor Hesselius. *March 26th, 1871*

My return to the schloss could not come soon enough, for I was sick with worrying over poor Carmilla. It had been barely three days, and yet it may well have seemed a lifetime.

Papa was waiting in the courtyard when our carriage arrived. He greeted us loudly, and joyously hugged all three of us ladies. It was only as I enquired as to the whereabouts of Carmilla, that his countenance changed.

I broke free from his embrace, and hitching up my skirts raced into the house and up the main staircase, calling out her name continuously as I proceeded along the corridor towards her bedroom. I think that in my heart I knew I would not find her.

Papa found me, sitting on the edge of Carmilla's bed, clutching her hairbrush to my breast. Wisps of brown hair were tufted around the bristles. The sweet scent of the girl I loved remained, lingering on the brush hairs. If I closed my eyes I could almost sense her sitting alongside me.

Papa sat down beside me and began to narrate a story which sounded both absurd and also wholly possible, if such a contradiction is feasible.

The events he described, when given consideration regarding the timings of my own affliction, indeed seemed to give a certain weight to their proceedings. Especially when given those assertions had been made by learned men such as Baron Vordenburg, and Doctor Alvinci.

As Papa explained all to me, I started to sob.

He tried his best to console me, convinced my crying and bouts of uncontrollable shaking was being brought on by the realisation of the danger I had unwittingly faced.

He would not have understood how, with his every word, the warmth left my body, leaving only a chill inside and a helpless feeling of immeasurable loss.

That night, before I slept, the priest had once again performed certain solemn rites, the purport of which I did not understand any more than I comprehended the reason for much of what had occurred over these last weeks.

I began to see more clearly a few days later. The disappearance of Carmilla was followed by the discontinuance of my nightly sufferings.

You have no doubt heard about the appalling superstition that prevails in Upper and Lower Styria, in Moravia, Silesia, Turkish Serbia, Poland, even Russia; the superstition, so we must call it, of the vampire.

If human testimony, taken with every care and solemnity, judicially, before commissions innumerable, each consisting of many members, all chosen for integrity and intelligence, constituting reports more voluminous perhaps than exist upon any one other class of cases, is worth anything, it is difficult to deny, or even to doubt the existence of such a phenomenon as the vampire.

For my part, I have heard no theory by which to explain what I have witnessed and experienced other than that supplied by the ancient and well-attested beliefs, which are asserted to such creatures.

You may suppose I write all this with composure. Far from it; I cannot think of it without agitation. Nothing but your earnest desire, so repeatedly and often expressed, could have induced me to sit down to a task that has unstrung my nerves for months to come, and reintroduced a shadow of the unspeakable horror which years after my deliverance continued to make my days and nights dreadful, and solitude insupportably terrifying.

Let me, if I may, add a word or two about that quaint Baron Vordenburg, to whose curious lore we were indebted for the discovery of much regarding the Countess Mircalla.

He had taken up his abode in Gratz. Where, living upon a mere pittance, at least in comparison to that which would have been afforded him by the once princely estates of his family, in Upper Styria, he devoted himself to the minute and laborious investigation of the marvellously authenticated traditions of the arcane, including that of vampirism.

He had at his fingers' ends all the great and little works upon such subjects.

"Magia Posthuma," "Phlegon de Mirabilibus," "Augustinus de cura pro Mortuis," "Philosophicae et Christianae Cogitationes de Vampiris," by John Christofer Herenberg; and a thousand others, among which I remember only a few of those which he lent to my father. He had a voluminous digest of all the judicial cases, from which he had extracted a system of principles that appear to govern—some always, and others occasionally only—the condition of the vampire. I may mention, in passing, that the deadly pallor attributed to that sort of revenants, is a mere melodramatic fiction. They present in the grave, and should they so desire, also when they show themselves in human society, the appearance of healthy life.

How they escape from their graves and return to them for certain hours every day, without displacing the clay or leaving any trace of disturbance in the state of the coffin or the cerements, has always been admitted to be utterly inexplicable. The amphibious existence of the vampire is sustained by daily renewed slumber in the grave. Its horrible lust for living blood supplies the vigour of its waking existence. The vampire is said to be prone to be fascinated with an engrossing vehemence, resembling the passion of love, toward particular persons. In pursuit of these it will exercise inexhaustible patience and stratagem, for access to a particular object may be obstructed in a hundred ways. It will never desist until it has satiated its passion, and drained the very life of its coveted victim. This may be true, but how can we be so sure such creatures are unable to love?

Vampires will, it is said, in these cases where they feel so compelled, husband and protract their murderous enjoyment with the refinement of an epicure, and heighten it by the gradual approaches of an artful courtship. In these cases it seems they yearn for something like sympathy and consent. In ordinary ones they go direct to the object of their craving, overpower with violence, and strangle and exhaust often at a single feast.

The vampire is a creature of an obsessively compulsive nature, and is apparently subject, in certain situations, to special conditions. In the particular instance of which I have given you a relation, Mircalla seemed to be limited to a name which, if not her real one, should at least reproduce, without the omission or addition of a single letter, those, as we say, anagrammatically, which compose it. Carmilla did this; so did Millarca.

My father, it turned out, is distantly related to the Baron Vordenburg, who remained with us for two or three weeks after the incidents at the Karnstein chapel. During his stay, my father asked the Baron about the story of the Moravian nobleman, and the vampire at Karnstein churchyard. The Baron's face puckered up into a mysterious smile; he looked down, still smiling on his worn spectacle case and fumbled with it. Then looking up, he said:

"I now have many journals and other papers written by that remarkable man; the most curious among them is one treating of the visit of which you speak, to Karnstein. The tradition of course, discolours and distorts a little. He might have been termed a Moravian nobleman, for he had changed his abode to that territory, and was indeed a noble. But he was, in truth, a native of Upper Styria.

"It is enough to say that in very early youth he had been a passionate and favoured lover of the beautiful Mircalla, Countess Karnstein. Her early death plunged him into inconsolable grief. It is the nature of vampires to increase and multiply, but only according to an ascertained and ghostly law.

"Assume, at starting, a territory perfectly free from that pest. How does it begin, and how does it multiply itself? I will tell you. A person, more or less wicked, puts an end to himself. A suicide, under certain circumstances becomes a vampire. That spectre visits living people in their slumbers; they die, and almost invariably, in the grave, develop into vampires. This happened in the case of the beautiful Mircalla, who was haunted by one of those demons. The Moravian, if that is the title you prefer to bestow upon him, soon discovered this, and in the course of the studies, to which he devoted himself, learned a great deal more.

"Among other things, he concluded that suspicion of vampirism would probably fall, sooner or later, upon the dead Countess, who in life had been his idol. He conceived a horror, be she what she might, of her remains being profaned by the outrage of a posthumous execution. He has left a curious paper to, so he asserts, prove that the vampire, on its expulsion from its amphibious existence, is projected into a far more horrible life; and he resolved to save his once beloved Mircalla from this.

"He adopted the stratagem of a journey here, a pretended removal of her remains, and a real obliteration of her monument. When age had stolen upon him, and from the vale of years, he looked back on the scenes he was leaving, and he considered in a different spirit what he had done, and a horror took possession of him. He made the tracings and notes, mapping out conditions within the chapel, which then guided us to the very spot of her concealed tomb, and he then drew up a confession of the deception that he had practiced. If he had intended any further action in this matter, death prevented him; and it hence fell to us to uncover the lair of the beast. Though, as fate would ordain it, we were too late, the *wolf-men* did our work for us."

We talked a little more, and among other things he said was this:

"One sign of the vampire is the power of the hand. The slender hand of Mircalla closed like a vice of steel on the General's wrist when he raised the hatchet to strike. But its power is not confined to its grasp; it leaves numbness in the limb it seizes, which is slowly, if ever, recovered from. It is strange then that General Spielsdorf should have made such a brisk recuperation?"

This was true; the speed of the General's recovery had only been overtaken by the strangeness of his subsequent disappearance.

The last time that I saw the General, it was less than a week after I returned home, following my stay at Father Wagner's house. Father had ordered that I stay away from our injured guest, as he was still livid about the werewolf attack upon my person, for which he continued to blame his old friend. But the General was a good man, and furthermore he had saved my life, and at a great cost to himself, and so, early one morning, I crept quietly along the landing, and into the General's room.

It was still early, but the General had already risen. He greeted my surprise visit with a hearty hug and a kiss to my forehead. I was amazed as to the swiftness of his recovery, and enquired as to his rapid restoration, but he just claimed a strong constitution.

We talked for a while, and he apologised for the recklessness of having brought the wolves into our area of Styria, but explained that his actions were blinded by a desire for vengeance. He also lamented the loss of my father's friendship, something that he would have preferred to set right before his imminent departure. I told him that I should speak with my father, in an attempt to rectify their situation, and he thanked me, and wished me well.

Later that morning, Papa and I were strolling out by the moat, it was a most tranquil scene and I had hoped the situation may have presented where I was able to broach his concerns regarding the General.

Our idle conversation was stifled by a most alarming occurrence. Before us, we were confronted by a huge grey wolf, which moved out from within the boundaries of our own courtyard, carried on an easy gait.

The size of the animal left us with little doubt, this was no ordinary creature, and in all likelihood was of the type which the General had invited into our borders.

Father swiftly placed himself before me, although what little protection he may have afforded I do not know.

The creature stared at us, through familiar blue eyes, for barely a matter of seconds, before turning towards the forest and gently loping away.

"My God!" muttered my father, in a manner more befitting someone having made a grand discovery.

I was about to enquire as to the nature of his tone, but already he had turned and was on his heels into the schloss. I followed in pursuit, neither of us slowing until father had reached the door to the General's room.

We entered, only to find that the General was missing; although his entire wardrobe remained. A journal was discarded on the bed, its pages lay open. Father picked the book up and tucked it under his arm. Then he ordered a thorough search of the house and grounds.

It was less than two hours later, when Madame came into the study to tell my father that the General had not been recovered.

Papa barely lifted his gaze from the journal, but gave instruction to abandon the search.

I never once saw the General again.

That evening Madame Perrodon, Mademoiselle De Lafontaine, and myself were sitting in the drawing room, partaking of a cup of hot chocolate, and some fresh buns, when my father entered. The open journal was still clutched tightly in his hands, and a disconcerted look played on his face.

"Tell me," he asked, "did Carmilla possess a pale blue dress?"

We answered that to the best of our knowledge she did not, and Papa nodded accordingly.

"I suspected as much," he replied, and then, without any further discourse, he turned and hurried away.

With the onset of winter, my father decided to take me on a visit to Rome. We stayed until the spring, and then took a tour through the rest of Italy. We remained away for more than a year and after returned to England, as it was time; according to my father, that I discovered the motherland.

Barely three months had elapsed since our *homecoming*, when we received word that Mademoiselle De Lafontaine and Lukas Cerny were to be married, in Gratz, in two months time. Excitedly I pestered Papa, enquiring as to the date of our expected return, stirred as all young women are by the prospect of a wedding party. Papa replied that our finances, at present would not bear the cost of another trip to Europe. Instead, we sent our best wishes in a letter.

Two months ago, over ten years on since those dreadful events, Papa announced that he intended on taking a trip back to Austria. He felt that the tide of the years was rapidly flowing against him, and that he needed to make his return while his mind was willing and his body still able.

His fingers were wrapped tightly around General Spielsdorf's weathered old journal as he informed me of his plans, and so when he talked of 'making right a wrong, with a dear old friend,' I was left with little doubt as to his intentions.

Two weeks ago as I exited the rail station, having bid a fond farewell and God speed to my father. I headed toward the main thoroughfare, intent on hailing a Hansom Cab in which to return home. As I walked, I was passed by a carriage of notable splendour, and moving at far greater pace than was the norm along this road.

Two outriders preceded the carriage, and it was their dress uniform, which I did not recognise, along with their speed of approach, which first alerted me to the approaching travelling carriage of a person of rank.

I watched with fascination as the carriage passed by, hoping that I might glimpse a view of British Nobility. What I saw made my heart miss a beat. The face that looked from the carriage window was that of a black woman, her head covered by a brightly coloured turban. She nodded at me, with an inane grin fixed on her face. Then just as swiftly she was gone.

As the carriage disappeared along the highway, my thoughts returned to those years gone by, and the accident, on that day when I first met Carmilla.

I remembered it clearly, the unfortunate happening on the road outside our schloss. After that splendid carriage had been righted, and had left us to proceed on its journey, Mademoiselle De Lafontaine had told us of another traveller, who had stayed within the overturned vehicle. I recalled her words well.

"Did you remark a woman in the carriage," she had enquired, "one who did not get out, but only looked from the window? She was a black skinned woman, but not in any way of fare appearance. This woman was hideous, as were her mannerisms. She sat, nodding and grinning derisively, towards us ladies, her eyes gleaming with an unwarranted rage, and her teeth set as if in fury."

As I walked to the top of the road and hailed a Hansom Cab, Mademoiselle's words kept repeating, over and again in my head. Finally, by the time I was ready to retire to my bed for the night, I had convinced myself that once again it was just my overactive imagination playing tricks, searching for mystery and the fantastical where there was none. I have suffered in this way, often. I believe that my mind seeks out a continuation of past strangeness, maybe because of the conflicting emotions which the situation previously afforded me. Reconciliation with prior horrors would also be reconciliation with my *one true love.*

It was a long time, many years in fact, before the terror of the events to which I had been subjected began to subside, even slightly; and I have been forced to view many of my intervening years *through a glass darkly*. To this hour, the image of Carmilla returns to my memory with ambiguous alternations, sometimes the playful, languid, beautiful girl whom I loved, and, if I am honest, part of me still loves. Sometimes the writhing fiend I saw in the ruined church; and often, of late, from a reverie I have started, a feeling of strangulation gripping at my throat, and fancying that I hear the light step of Carmilla at the drawing room door.

Thank You for Reading

I would like to use this opportunity to say *'thank you'* to everyone who has taken time to read *Carmilla: The Wolves of Styria*.

I hope you have enjoyed this re-imagining of Joseph Sheridan Le Fanu's original novella, *Carmilla*. If so, then please consider sparing a few minutes to post a review on Amazon.com, or any other relevant sites. Reviews offer a valuable source of exposure for authors, and this is especially true for writers in the indie community. If you have enjoyed my writing and are interested in finding out more about my work, then please feel free to connect via one of the links posted below.

I thank you once again for your support and words of encouragement. It is greatly appreciated, always.

Best wishes.

David Brian.

http://www.davidbrianwriting.co.uk/index.html
https://www.goodreads.com/author/show/1068132.David_Brian
https://www.facebook.com/David-Brian-463536253659317/

Printed in Great Britain
by Amazon